W9-CJC-295

FOREVER'S PROMISE

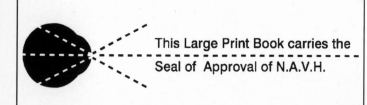

This Large Print Book carries the
Seal of Approval of N.A.V.H.

BAYOU DREAMS

FOREVER'S PROMISE

FARRAH ROCHON

THORNDIKE PRESS

A part of Gale, Cengage Learning

GALE
CENGAGE Learning·

Farmington Hills, Mich • San Francisco • New York • Waterville, Maine
Meriden, Conn • Mason, Ohio • Chicago

GALE
CENGAGE Learning®

Copyright © 2014 by Farrah Roybiskie.
Bayou Dreams Series #3.
Thorndike Press, a part of Gale, Cengage Learning.

ALL RIGHTS RESERVED

This is a work of fiction. Names, characters, places, and incidents are either the product of the author's imagination or are used fictitiously, and any resemblance to actual persons, living or dead, business establishments, events or locales is entirely coincidental.

Thorndike Press® Large Print African-American.
The text of this Large Print edition is unabridged.
Other aspects of the book may vary from the original edition.
Set in 16 pt. Plantin.

LIBRARY OF CONGRESS CATALOGING-IN-PUBLICATION DATA

Rochon, Farrah.
  Forever's promise / by Farrah Rochon. — Large print edition.
    pages ; cm. — (Thorndike Press large print African-American) (Bayou dreams series ; #3)
  ISBN 978-1-4104-6950-2 (hardcover) — ISBN 1-4104-6950-6 (hardcover)
  1. African Americans—Fiction. 2. Louisiana—Fiction. 3. Large type books. I. Title.
PS3618.O346F67 2014
813'.6—dc23   2014010540

Published in 2014 by arrangement with Harlequin Books, S.A.

Printed in Mexico
1 2 3 4 5 6 7 18 17 16 15 14

This one is for my fans!
My heartfelt thanks to all of you
for the years of support.

"In everything give thanks; for this is God's will for you in Christ Jesus."
— *1 Thessalonians* 5:18

CHAPTER 1

Shayla Kirkland swirled the cappuccino's foamy topping into the shape of an apple before handing the mug to her former tenth-grade Free Enterprise teacher.

"Here you go, Mr. Peterson. One nonfat cappuccino with extra foam."

"Well, look at that. Quite a fancy trick you've got there, Shayla," he said, taking a sip as he cast an appraising glance around the spacious coffeehouse. "It's nice to see that someone paid attention in class. We could use more homegrown businesses here in Gauthier."

"Of course I paid attention. Your class was one of my favorites."

"I'll bet you tell that to all your old teachers." He winked as he handed her a five-dollar bill.

Shayla dropped the change he waved off into the tip jar before wiping down the counter, then turned to the service window that led to the kitchen of The Jazzy Bean.

"Hey, Lucinda, are those salads ready?"

Lucinda Sullivan, who had been Shayla's late mother's best friend and had given Shayla her first sip of beer when she was twelve years old, placed two square salad bowls on the ledge of the little cutaway window.

When she'd made the spur-of-the-moment decision to open a coffeehouse in her hometown of Gauthier, Louisiana, Shayla hadn't given much thought to her plan — wholly uncharacteristic for her usually methodical self. The one thing she *did* know was that she wanted to include a café. After much begging and shameless pleading, Lucinda had mercifully accepted the job as cook. Shayla knew coffee. Her other culinary skills left much to be desired.

"I changed Harold's order to a grilled chicken salad instead of fried," Lucinda told her.

"Good woman," Shayla said.

She loaded the salads onto a tray, along with two glasses of sweet tea and mismatched cutlery she'd salvaged from the remnants of Armant's Antique Shop, which had occupied this building on downtown Gauthier's Main Street for decades before Shayla bought it.

As owner, her day was usually spent making sure the coffee shop was running smoothly, and maybe delivering the occasional order when things got busy during the lunch rush. But with two of her employees out sick today, Shayla found herself utilizing those skills she'd learned as a barista while putting herself through college.

She took the salads to the table where two of her regulars, Harold Porter and Nathan Robottom, sat engaged in a serious game of cards.

She placed their salads in front of them. "You gentlemen mind taking a short intermission?"

"Hey, what's this?" Harold asked. "I ordered a fried chicken salad."

Shayla crossed her arms and challenged him with her stare. She worked hard to keep a grin from emerging.

"Aw, c'mon," Harold groused. "It's bad enough you got me eating salads. Now I can't even get it with the chicken cooked the way I like?"

"The grilled tastes even better than the fried," Shayla said. "Trust me. If you don't think so, your salad is on the house."

Harold's lips pinched in a frown and he muttered something unintelligible, but

Shayla caught the telling crinkle at the corners of his eyes.

"You'd better be happy you're pretty," he said. "I wouldn't give up fried chicken for no ugly woman."

She laughed, giving him a good-natured pat on the back before leaving the men to their meal.

When she'd settled on the concept for The Jazzy Bean she decided her coffeehouse would not contribute to the failing health of any patrons with known medical conditions. Harold was just one of several customers who suffered from high blood pressure. If he wanted to dine on oily, fatty, heart-attack-inducing food, he would have to go elsewhere.

Shayla came upon a table of teachers from the local high school. They routinely dropped in on Monday evenings for conversation and coffee.

"How's it going, ladies? Is that car still giving you trouble, Denise?"

Denise Lewis, who graduated from Gauthier High with her brother, Braylon, waved off her concern. "My car is fine." With a sly grin, she added, "Although I do feel a little tummy ache coming on. I think I need a trip to the emergency room."

The table of women burst into laughter.

12

Shayla's brow dipped in a curious frown as she eyed the boisterous crew. "Okay, what am I missing?"

"Oh, don't mind her." Bianca Charles, who'd served on the student council with her back when Shayla was in the tenth grade, motioned toward Denise. "She's just trying to come up with a reason to see that fine new E.R. doctor over at Maplesville General."

Denise flattened her palm against her chest. "I don't need to fake being sick. I damn near have a heart attack whenever I see him."

Shayla rolled her eyes. "Let me know if you ladies need anything else. More coffee, scones, CPR?"

They erupted in more laughter.

"I'll take another cup of coffee," Denise said, scooting off her stool and following Shayla to the counter.

"I'll take one, too," her best friend, Paxton Jones, called from the table she'd commandeered over in the corner.

"Still not talking to you," Shayla said.

"Why aren't you talking to Paxton?" Denise asked. "You two were joined at the hip in high school."

"Because I took a job in Little Rock," Paxton explained as she walked over to the

13

counter and held out her coffee cup. "You'd think my dearest friend in the world would be happy for me."

"Not gonna happen," Shayla said, reluctantly refilling the mug with the medium roast she'd recently brewed.

Paxton took a sip before she said, "Someone here seems to forget that *she* left *me* first, and she went all the way to the West Coast. You didn't see me getting all surly."

"Big difference. I didn't have a choice. I had a scholarship and then an internship that led to a job. This isn't even a promotion for you. It's a lateral move. You don't have to leave if you don't want to."

Paxton came around the counter and pinched her cheek. "I still love you, Shayla. Despite the fact that you're acting like a big, curly-haired baby."

She knew she was being a baby. Petty and selfish, too. But she'd learned of her best friend's impending move only a few hours ago. Shayla figured she deserved at least another day to wallow and complain before congratulating her.

"You still coming over tonight?" Shayla asked.

"Can I take a rain check?" Paxton motioned to the table, scattered with spreadsheets and forms and other reminders of the hectic corporate lifestyle Shayla had once lived.

She tried to suppress the surge of envy that gripped her. That fast-paced, cutthroat world was no longer a part of her existence. The Jazzy Bean, her nieces — *they* were her life now.

"It's probably better we meet tomorrow," Shayla said. "My neighbor is babysitting for me. I need to pick the girls up and get them ready for bed."

"When does Leslie get back?"

"Tomorrow night. She decided to stay an extra day in Houston to spend time with her extended family."

"Good. It gives you more time with the girls," Paxton said.

"Except I've had to spend all my extra time here in the coffee shop," Shayla pointed out. "And you know I can use all the extra bonding time I can get, especially with Cassidy."

Paxton frowned and patted Shayla's arm. "It'll get better. Just give it time."

"Yeah, that's what I keep telling myself," Shayla said.

By the time Lucinda turned the Open sign to Closed, just after 6:00 p.m., Shayla was ready to dive headfirst into bed.

"Get out of here and get some rest," Lucinda said. "I'll close up."

"If I had enough energy I would kiss you," Shayla told her. She'd worked on the corporate side of the coffee business for so long she'd forgotten just how exhausting the day-to-day operations of a coffee shop could be.

The rest she so desperately craved would have to wait, because for the first time in nearly two decades, she was responsible for someone other than herself. After months of campaigning, she'd finally convinced her sister-in-law, Leslie, to leave her two nieces, eight-year-old Cassidy and three-year-old Kristi, in her care while Leslie attended her cousin's wedding in Houston this past weekend.

Reconnecting with her family and getting to know her sister-in-law and nieces better was the chief impetus behind Shayla's impulsive move back to Louisiana following her younger brother's premature death. Over the past eight months, she had discovered that their frayed family fabric was not as easily mended as she'd hoped, especially when she'd played such a huge part in tearing said family fabric.

But things were slowly getting better. The fact that Leslie had entrusted Shayla with Kristi and Cassidy — even if it was just for four days — spoke volumes about how

16

much their relationship had improved.

Shayla bade Lucinda good-night before leaving her to lock up. She headed left on Main Street's newly refurbished brick-laid sidewalk — just one of the outcomes of the downtown area's recent restoration projects. Her house, which she'd purchased in a package deal when she'd bought the building that housed The Jazzy Bean, was located in the residential neighborhood adjacent to Main Street.

On the short five-minute walk home, Shayla took in the sweet smell of the night jasmine that grew in the window boxes outside Lizzie's Consignment Shop. The balmy summer night was so different from what she'd become accustomed to in the Pacific Northwest, but she embraced it.

It was strange — after living on the West Coast for nearly twenty years she'd anticipated bouts of homesickness after packing up her condo in Seattle, but they'd never materialized. Instead, Shayla had been overwhelmed by the sense of peace and belonging she'd experienced when she'd returned to Gauthier.

She'd lived in Seattle for much of her adult life, but *this* was home.

She walked past her house and went next door. Her neighbor Gayle Martin had offered to babysit her nieces so they wouldn't be stuck in the back room at The Jazzy Bean after they got home from school today. Shayla had had every intention of meeting them at the bus stop and spending quality time with the girls, but her busy workday couldn't be helped, not with both Erin, the college student she'd hired a couple of months ago, and her manager, Desiree, calling in sick.

She went around to the back door of Gayle's wood-framed creole cottage, which was almost an exact replica of hers. The only difference was the color. Shayla had painted her house a deep brick-red and added stark-white shutters. It stood out from the white and pastel homes in the neighborhood.

She rapped twice on the door before going inside. "Knock, knock," she called. "Anybody home?"

Gayle came into the kitchen, Shayla's nieces trailing behind.

"Hey, Aunt Shayla," Kristi greeted with an excited wave. Her hands were stained myriad colors.

"What happened here? Did a rainbow try to eat your fingers?" She playfully tugged Kristi's ponytail.

"More like the Easter Bunny," Gayle said. "We've been dyeing eggs."

18

"Ah, that also explains the wardrobe change." Shayla gestured to the oversize Jimi Hendrix T-shirts both girls wore.

"I didn't want them staining their school uniforms, so I drafted a couple of my son's old shirts."

"Yikes. I hope they weren't his favorites."

Gayle gave a halfhearted shrug. "Serves him right for leaving them here. I've been telling him to come get his stuff for ten years."

Gathering the girls' backpacks and neatly folded school uniforms from the table, Shayla said, "Thanks again for watching them on such short notice." She waved goodbye as she ushered the kids out the back door.

They were halfway across the yard when Gayle called to them. "Wait a minute." She came over, carrying a slim cardboard package and a carton of eggs. "Here's the second dye kit and the rest of the eggs. They're already boiled. I told the girls that maybe you'd dye a few with them tonight."

Shayla managed a weak smile, squelching a groan at Kristi's excited expression. She was having a hard enough time handling basic child care; she could not pull off arts and crafts, especially after the day she'd endured.

"Maybe later." Like when her sister-in-law came home tomorrow.

They continued across the side lawn between her house and Gayle's. She made a mental note to call the high school kid she'd hired to cut her lawn. The clover patches were ankle-deep. Then again, maybe she should leave the grass uncut and hold an Easter-egg hunt for the girls. That should score her some points in the cool aunt department, right?

"So, did you two have fun?" Shayla asked.

Kristi's ponytail bounced up and down with her enthusiastic head nod, but Cassidy barely responded.

Shayla curbed the sigh that nearly escaped. In the eight months since she'd returned to Gauthier her chief goal had been to form a relationship with her nieces. To her utter disappointment, things were not going as planned. Kristi had warmed up to her after the first time Shayla had taken them out for ice cream, but it would take far more than a double scoop of chocolate-chip-cookie dough to break down Cassidy's walls.

Her reluctance had only prodded Shayla to try harder. She would win Cassidy over. She owed it to her baby brother to forge a relationship with the family he'd left behind.

Shayla suffered through the familiar ache that struck her chest whenever she thought about Braylon. She pulled in a deep breath and slowly let it out, willing the threatening tears to remain at bay. She knew better than to let her mind wander there, especially when she was so drained. She would *not* lose it in front of the girls.

Shayla unlocked the door to the quaint, two-bedroom cottage, which surprisingly suited her just as much as her condo in a high-rise building in downtown Seattle had. She let the girls enter ahead of her, then locked the door behind them.

"Aunt Shayla?"

She nearly stumbled at the sound of Cassidy's soft voice. Another thing she could count on one hand was the number of times her eldest niece had addressed her directly.

Shayla walked over and ran a tentative hand along Cassidy's bouncy curls that were so much like her own. "Yes, Cass?"

"Can we dye the rest of the eggs?"

Shayla's shoulders fell. Why, of all things, did she have to ask that?

"Oh, honey, I've been up since 4:00 a.m. I'm too tired to dye eggs right now." She lifted a curl. "I'll tell you what. If you and your sister watch one of your DVDs while I take a nap, we'll dye the eggs a bit later. Is that okay?"

Cassidy nodded, but Shayla caught the disappointment in her eyes.

Great. The one time her niece asks for something, and she comes off feeling like the auntie from hell. But if she tried dyeing Easter eggs right now they would all end up looking like Kristi's fingers.

She allowed the girls to pick a movie out of the collection of DVDs her sister-in-law had left for them. Once they were both settled on the rug in front of the television, she went into her bedroom, kicked off her tennis shoes, and crashed face-first on top of the still-made bed.

She wasn't sure how much time had passed when she heard a faint voice call, "Aunt Shayla?"

She stirred, turning over and curling into a fetal position.

"Aunt Shayla, something's wrong with Kristi."

"What is it, baby?" she murmured.

"Kristi's sick. She's throwing up. And it looks . . . funny."

Shayla blinked. Cassidy's words registered and she jerked up, hopping off the bed.

"Where is she?"

Cassidy pointed. "In the bathroom."

Shayla ran to the bathroom, her heart

jumping to her throat when she came upon her three-year-old niece. Kristi's shirt and the bathroom floor were covered in yellowish-orange vomit, and she was coughing, her thin frame jerking in violent fits and spurts.

"Oh, my God! What happened?"

Cassidy hunched her shoulders, her bottom lip trembling.

Was that bile? Was Kristi throwing up buckets of bile?

Oh, God.

She finally got the chance to look after the girls, and *this* happened? She'd be lucky if Leslie let her anywhere near them again.

She scooped Kristi into her arms and called for Cassidy over her shoulder. "Come on, Cass. Let's get her to the doctor."

Not wanting to waste time searching for tennis shoes, she slipped her feet into the slippers she'd left in the bathroom and grabbed her purse and car keys from the kitchen table where she'd dropped them earlier.

She suddenly remembered the medical authorization letter Leslie had given her before she'd left for Houston late Friday evening, just in case something happened. Not once did Shayla anticipate actually using it.

She snatched the letter from where she'd tacked it to the refrigerator, next to the list of emergency numbers Leslie had also insisted Shayla have at the ready. She considered calling her sister-in-law, but what would she tell her? She didn't even know what was going on yet. She needed to get Kristi to the hospital ASAP. Then she'd call Leslie.

Gauthier didn't have a hospital. In fact, the town had only recently acquired a health clinic that was staffed by volunteer doctors and nurses a couple of days a week. Thankfully, Maplesville, which was only twenty minutes away — fifteen if she didn't hear any beeps on the police radar detector mounted to her dashboard — had a small hospital.

Shayla strapped Kristi into her booster seat and told Cassidy to buckle her seatbelt. Once she was behind the wheel, she maneuvered the rearview mirror so that she could see her nieces.

"Don't worry, everything's going to be okay," Shayla assured them.

God, she hoped she was right.

"Do you feel any tenderness or pain when I press here?" Xavier Wright asked the twenty-something who'd walked into the E.R. with

24

complaints of stomach pains.

"Not really," she said. "Maybe a little higher."

He gently pressed along her rib cage. "Here?"

"Just a little higher," she said, adding a seductive purr to her voice.

Xavier bit back a curse. His teeth gritted as he backed away from the exam table. He didn't have time to perform a breast exam, even though he knew that's exactly what his latest "patient" had in mind.

"I don't think this is appendicitis," he said. "You may want to try a laxative."

Her forehead scrunched as she frowned. Yeah, mentioning laxatives was always a good way to zap the sexy out of any conversation.

Xavier made a couple of notations in the patient's electronic chart. "I'll send a nurse in to discuss some over-the-counter medications that may help."

"Don't bother," she said with a pout.

"It's up to you whether or not you heed my medical advice," he said, disregarding her disgruntled huff. He had zero tolerance for this kind of nonsense today.

As he backed out of the exam room, he spotted his favorite RN, Patricia Reyes, exiting the room across the hallway. She gestured to the room he'd just escaped from. "You figure out what was bothering that hot little thing in there?"

"According to her, it's stomach pains," Xavier answered.

"Yeah, right. I think she's suffering from Horny Woman Syndrome. It's been going around since a certain doctor pulled into town."

Xavier pitched his head back and massaged the bridge of his nose. "I swear I'm not doing anything to encourage them."

"You don't have to, darling. You're young, single, handsome *and* a doctor. You're like a virus that every desperate woman within a twenty-mile radius wants to catch."

"Thanks. That makes me feel a lot better."

Patricia's laughter followed him as he made his way to the small employees' lounge and poured himself a cup of six-hour-old coffee. He didn't bother with sugar or cream; this was purely for survival. He'd pulled a double shift and was dead on his feet.

The door opened and Bruce Saunders, who was currently one of only two permanent E.R. physicians at Maplesville General, walked in.

"How's it going?" Bruce asked. "I heard

you had another female patient with a mysterious ailment who refused to see any doctor but Dr. Wright."

Xavier held his hands out, exasperation weighing his shoulders down. "In the month that I've been here I swear that's the tenth woman who's managed to get past triage with some trumped-up illness."

"This place hasn't been this busy in a while." Bruce chuckled, pouring himself a cup of the stale coffee. "At least some good has come from it. Yesterday, Patricia discovered that Etta Mae Watson had a staph infection on the back of her leg that she knew nothing about. Chasing after you probably saved her life."

The door opened again, and another of the nurses said, "We have two patients waiting. A vomiting three-year-old and Jackson Pritchard with chest pains."

"I'll take Mr. Pritchard," Bruce said. "I had to crack his chest open a couple of years ago."

"He's behind trauma curtain three. Dr. Wright, I put the three-year-old in the private exam room."

Xavier downed the rest of his lukewarm coffee in one gulp and headed out of the lounge. At least he didn't have to worry about a three-year-old faking an illness in hopes of being seen by the shiny new doctor.

He punched the number the nurse gave him into his electronic tablet and pulled up the patient's chart before entering the room. The younger of two little girls was seated on the exam table. Her mother stood to the left of her, rubbing a soothing hand along the little girl's back. One side of her shirt was streaked with a yellowish substance.

"What do we have here?" Xavier asked.

"I don't know what's going on with her," the mom said. The slight tremble in her voice betrayed the anxiety she was likely trying to hide for the sake of her daughters.

Xavier waited for her to catch his gaze. "It's going to be okay," he said. "We'll take care of her."

The mother nodded, though her eyes teemed with distress.

"Let's have a look." He leaned the child back on the table and lightly pressed her stomach. Her face contorted and she sat up straight. Xavier backed away just in time. She unloaded brilliant yellow vomit all over the floor and her hospital gown.

"There she goes again," the older girl said.

"How many times has she vomited?" Xavier asked the mother as he grabbed a clean hospital gown from a small closet and ripped off the plastic. He lifted the soiled gown and draped the fresh one over the girl.

"I'm not sure," the mother said.

She looked to the older child, who said in a soft voice, "Three times, I think."

"So this would make four," the mother said. "No, five. Someone needs to clean the parking lot outside."

Xavier sent her a reassuring smile. "I'll let maintenance know."

"Is it bile?" the mother asked. "She's vomiting bile, isn't she?"

"Nah, it's not bile," Xavier said. He dipped his head, bringing it to eye level with the toddler. "What I want to know is why is it such a pretty color? Have you been eating candy?"

The little girl shook her head.

"You sure?" Xavier asked.

"I promise," she said in a thready whisper.

The mother plopped a hand on her forehead. "Oh, God. I know what it is." She looked to the older girl. "Did you two try dyeing eggs?" The question was met with complete silence. "Cassidy, I told you to wait until I woke from my nap." She turned his attention to him. "I should have suspected this from the start."

Xavier's bullshit meter started to buzz. He wasn't the world's greatest parenting expert, but this seemed sketchy. What mother would leave two young children unsupervised with egg-dyeing materials in plain view?

"Were you using regular food coloring, or was it one of those egg-dyeing kits?" Xavier asked the mother.

"It's a kit."

"It's probably nontoxic, but you'll need to check the packaging just to make sure." He stooped to the little girl's eye level. "I'm going to get Nurse Patricia to give you some medicine. It will make you throw up again, but then I promise you'll feel a lot better."

The mother's shoulders wilted in relief. She ran a hand along the little girl's arm.

Xavier had not seen a phonier display of concern since he arrived in Maplesville. It pissed him off, because she'd had him going there for a moment with her fearful, worried act.

He straightened back to his full height and addressed the mother. "Mom, can I speak to you out in the hallway?"

A moment's confusion flashed across her face before she shook her head and said, "I'm Kristi's aunt, not her mom."

Even worse. Using her niece.

"The hallway?" Xavier repeated, motioning to the door. "Wait here one minute," he said once they'd exited the room. He went over to the nurse's station and relayed orders to Patricia, then gestured for the aunt to follow him to the small alcove that housed the vending machines and a water fountain.

As soon as they were out of earshot of the rest of the E.R.'s occupants, he turned and said, "The only reason I'm not calling child protective services is because your niece will be fine once the ipecac makes her throw up the rest of the dye she ingested, but pull something like this again and I'll have CPS out here before you can blink."

The woman's head reared back. "*Excuse me?*"

"Feeding a three-year-old dye?"

Her eyes grew wide. "You think *I* gave her the dye?"

"Don't even try it." Xavier crossed his arms over his chest, a disdainful sneer on his lips. "The women in this town have done some outrageous things to get into my E.R., but you came very close to crossing a line."

Her expression morphed from shock to rage.

"Are you serious? You think I tried to poison my own niece just to meet you?" She waved her hands down the front of her body. "Do I look like I'm on the prowl for a

31

damn man?"

Xavier took a moment to study her appearance, from her hair, that looked as if she had just gotten out of bed, to the vomit-covered T-shirt and Minnie Mouse house slippers on her feet. She hadn't bothered with fancy clothes and the full makeup routine as the other women who'd come here trying to hit on him. She looked like someone who'd grabbed a sick child and hauled ass to the E.R.

Her beautiful dark brown eyes became murderous as she stepped up to him.

"Look, you egotistical asshole. I can't speak for the other women in this town, but let me make one thing clear. Meeting you was the *last* thing on my mind when I stepped into this E.R. I didn't even know you would be in this E.R. Do you really think I would endanger my own niece on the off chance that you might be working today?"

Her chest rose and fell with the sharp breaths she sucked in following her fiery tirade. Rage had her nostrils flaring, those brown eyes intense and full of fury.

It was a magnificent sight to behold.

"I don't know who you think you are," she said, "but you are not all that, Dr. Wright. Not even close."

She looked him up and down, as if he was a nasty wad of gum she'd found stuck to the bottom of her shoe.

"I'm sorry," Xavier started. "I —"

She put her hand up. "Save it. And do *not* follow me back to that exam room. I don't want you anywhere near my niece."

Xavier tried to speak, but found himself at a loss for words as he watched her stomp back to the exam room.

He also found himself slightly aroused.

The realization came as such a shock that, for a moment, it left him paralyzed, unable to do anything but stare at the faux-wood exam room door that had just shut behind her. He should be appalled by his body's reaction.

Instead, Xavier briefly closed his eyes and soaked in the feeling.

It had been so damn long since he'd felt *any*thing. He needed to savor this. He wanted to remember it when he was sitting at home, alone, trying to recall what it felt like to have that kind of passion flowing through his veins.

CHAPTER 2

Shayla pulled her Volvo coupe under the detached aluminum carport next to her side kitchen door, but she didn't move. Instead, she let the engine idle as she continued to grip the steering wheel with both hands. There had been utter silence throughout the entire twenty-minute drive from the hospital in Maplesville. She'd spent most of the ride sending up prayers of thanks that Kristi's condition had turned out to be nothing serious.

She'd spent the remainder of the ride trying to quell her rage over that cocky E.R. doctor and the ridiculous conclusion he'd jumped to. As if she would ever do something so desperate.

Her annoyance only grew when she realized he must be the new doctor all the teachers were foaming at the mouth over at The Jazzy Bean earlier that day. No wonder Mr. Conceited had made such an outrageous assumption. After the talk she'd overheard at the coffeehouse, she wouldn't put it past some of the women to go to such lengths.

Shayla didn't care how gorgeous he was — and, don't get her wrong, he was gorgeous — but she would never put her niece in danger just to score an introduction. She may have been thunderstruck by those whiskey-brown eyes the moment he'd stepped into the exam room, but she wasn't *that* desperate.

After she'd put the cocky doctor in his place, they'd remained at the hospital for another half hour, until Kristi had vomited twice more. The nurse had given her fluids to guard against dehydration and sent them home with instructions to give her Gatorade and keep the egg dye out of children's reach.

Someone shouldn't have had to tell her that. It should have been a given. As excited as they were about dyeing the eggs, she should have known the girls would do something like this.

But, then again, what did she know about kids?

"You are *so* in over your head," she muttered. Shayla released a deep, tired breath as she cut the engine and opened the door.

She went to the back passenger side and unstrapped a sleeping Kristi from her car seat. Hefting the toddler into her arms, Shayla whispered to Cassidy, "Let's get in the house."

She recoiled at the thought of having to reprimand her niece, but Shayla knew it had to be done. She'd given specific instructions that the dye was not to be touched until she woke up. It was bad enough that they'd disobeyed, but being the eldest, Cassidy should have known better than to allow her little sister to put the dye anywhere near her mouth.

Of course, the ultimate responsibility fell to her. *She* was the adult in charge. It didn't matter that she was tired enough to fall asleep this very second; she should have been paying attention to the girls, not napping.

Shayla carried Kristi into the guest bedroom and undressed her, taking care not to wake her. She used a warm washcloth to wipe her down, then took a page from Gayle's book and dressed her in the old, worn USC Trojans T-shirt she'd had since freshman year. Other than a little squirming, Kristi hardly moved. The poor baby was exhausted. Shayla could sympathize.

When she returned to the kitchen, Cassidy was sitting at the table, picking at the bright blue fingernail polish she'd painted on this past Saturday during their pamper party — another of Shayla's attempts to connect with her nieces. Only the light above the stove illuminated the room.

"Do you want some juice?" Shayla asked, grabbing two glasses from the cupboard and a bottle of cranberry juice from the refrigerator. Cassidy shook her head, but Shayla filled the glass halfway and set it in front of her, anyway.

She took the chair opposite her niece, placed both elbows on the table and massaged her temples. She wasn't even sure how to begin this conversation.

Since she'd returned to Gauthier with some half-formed idea to help her sister-in-law raise her nieces, she could count on her fingers the number of times Cassidy had spoken to her without considerable prompting. Over the past three days, she'd opened up several times, even joining Shayla and Kristi in an impromptu karaoke concert Saturday night. Shayla didn't want to hinder the small bit of progress she'd made with Cassidy by coming down on her with a heavy lecture.

But she couldn't allow what had happened tonight to just slide. She wasn't here to

37

make friends with an eight-year-old; she was here to help raise her. Disciplinarian was part of the job description.

"Cass, didn't I tell you that we would dye the eggs later?" Shayla started.

Pulling her trembling bottom lip between her teeth, Cassidy nodded.

"Your sister could have been seriously hurt if those dyes were toxic. You know better than to put them in your mouth, but Kristi doesn't. This could have been very, very bad, Cassidy."

Dread cascaded down Shayla's spine just thinking about what *could* have happened. Goodness, how did parents do this 24/7 for eighteen years? It had been just over three days and she was ready to climb the walls.

"Promise me you won't disobey in the future," Shayla said.

"I promise," Cassidy mumbled. The dour frown on her face told Shayla that the little headway she'd made in softening Cass's feelings toward her had just evaporated. Great.

"Why don't you get ready for bed," Shayla said. "You have school tomorrow, and it's already past your bedtime."

Cass remained stoic as she rose and lumbered down the narrow hallway toward the bedrooms. Shayla remained at the kitchen table, sipping her cranberry juice and trying to talk herself out of adding vodka to the glass. She'd messed up once already tonight. She knew better than to render herself completely incapacitated by drinking alcohol while the girls were still under her watch.

She set the glass on the table and covered her face with both hands.

"What in the hell have you gotten yourself into?"

She had never been the type to make rash decisions. Her careful, methodical thinking had taken her from being a lowly junior marketing assistant to the executive director of community relations at one of the country's largest coffeehouse chains. Yet she'd succumbed to the impulsive decision to return to her hometown, turning her once well-ordered life completely upside down. What on earth had possessed her to do that?

"You know exactly what brought you back here," Shayla whispered before downing the last of her juice in one gulp.

Guilt.

Suffocating, unrelenting, soul-crushing guilt. And if leaving her previous life behind so she could do right by her brother's family was the only way to assuage that smothering guilt, then so be it.

Shayla set the juice glasses in the sink, made sure the back door was locked and went in to check on the girls. Kristi was still sound asleep. Cassidy was in bed, reading an R. L. Stein Goosebumps book.

A smile drew across Shayla's lips. Like father, like daughter. Braylon had kept stacks of Bobbsey Twins mystery paperbacks next to his bed when he was younger.

Why did you leave these two babies?

How she wished she could ask him that question face-to-face.

It took some effort to swallow past the lump that instantly formed in her throat. Once she was able to clear it, she said, "Ten more minutes, okay, Cass?" The girl nodded. "Good night. I love you, honey."

Cassidy didn't respond.

Shayla's eyes closed briefly in defeat before she pulled the door, leaving a five-inch gap. She went into her bedroom and barely managed to change into her own old, comfortable T-shirt before falling onto the bed and into a deep sleep.

The next morning, Shayla was nearly a half hour late making it to The Jazzy Bean. Unlike yesterday, Gayle had not been there to help get Kristi and Cass off to school. She'd enjoyed her first weekend alone with the girls, but she would probably weep in relief when Leslie picked them up tonight.

It was no surprise that Lucinda had everything running like a well-oiled machine by the time Shayla arrived at The Jazzy Bean. And, thank God, Erin was back behind the counter.

"I am so happy to see you," Shayla told her, giving her a brief hug. "It's been a long time since I've had to run the front end of a coffeehouse on my own."

"I probably could have come in yesterday afternoon, but I wanted to make sure I was completely over the virus before I returned to work."

"Good girl," Shayla said. "Spoken like a future pediatrician."

"I talked to Desiree this morning. She's still in the don't-stray-too-far-from-the-bathroom phase." Erin grimaced. "Believe me, you don't want her here."

"Lucinda and I did okay yesterday. We can handle it now that you're back," Shayla said.

Despite wanting to run from the building screaming during yesterday's lunchtime rush, for the most part she'd enjoyed being back in the thick of things. She wasn't about to give up Erin and Desiree — not by a long shot — but at the end of the day Shayla had felt a sense of accomplishment she hadn't experienced since her early days with her old company, when she was still climbing her way up the bottom rungs of the ladder.

The morning crowd mostly consisted of regulars, with a smattering of unknown faces that stopped in on their way to the site of the new concrete plant being built just off Highway 190 a few towns over. One of the contractors had stumbled upon The Jazzy Bean a few weeks ago and bought coffee for the rest of his crew. It had become a ritual. Someone came in at least three days a week, ordering one of the carryout cartons that held a gallon of coffee.

That thought brought up another one.

Shayla looked over from where she was adding bagels to the tray inside the display case. "Hey, Erin, will you be able to deliver coffee to the clinic this morning?"

"Not unless you want to make the drinks," Erin called over the noise of the coffee grinder.

"I don't think so," Shayla said. Yesterday had exposed her limits. Although she still had some skills behind the espresso machine, when it came to barista duties, Erin was far superior.

She was really missing Desiree right about now. Her manager was the one who usually slipped out during the slow period to bring coffee to the health clinic.

Since its doors opened about two months before, The Jazzy Bean had provided free coffee and breakfast pastries to the doctors and nurses who volunteered at the clinic that had been the brainchild of local attorney turned state senator, Matthew Gauthier. Matt had recently won his position in a special election and, in a surprise to no one, had quickly set out to improve life in Gauthier.

Residents could receive health screenings and checkups for a nominal fee, which Shayla learned was code for "whatever folks could afford to pay." The supplies were bought using donations, and the medical professionals donated their time. Shayla figured providing a light breakfast was the very least she could do.

She filled a travel carton with today's dark roast and prepared a large cup with decaf for the one nurse who didn't drink regular. She grabbed a plastic tray and loaded it with the oatmeal, cranberry and flaxseed breakfast bars she ordered from the organic bakery in New Orleans that supplied her healthier pastries. She was still having a hard time convincing customers to try the heart-healthy food selections, but Shayla claimed a small victory every time someone got on board.

The clinic was an easy walk, only a couple of blocks down, in a single-story bungalow on Cooper Lane once owned by Matt Gauthier's family.

She walked up the front steps and encountered Tanya Miller exiting the clinic. Tanya had lived directly across the street from the house Shayla had grown up in, where Leslie now lived with the girls. She was accompanied by a teenager who looked as if he'd come out on the losing end of a battle with the flu.

"Hey there, Shayla," Tanya said, holding the door open for her. "I was just on my way to your place to get some soup. I hope Lucinda has chicken noodle on the menu today."

"Chicken and rice."

"Close enough," Tanya said. "Maybe I'll be able to get this one to eat something."

"Good luck with that," Shayla said, eyeing the boy. She entered the clinic and called out a hello to the half-dozen people seated in folding chairs in the lobby.

"Shayla! How are you?" Shayla turned to find Malinda Donaldson walking toward her. Malinda was once a friendly rival on the Maplesville Mustangs' Quiz Bowl team. The Gauthier High Lions had never lost a single match to them throughout Shayla's high school career. Yes, she had been a nerd. And she was damn proud of it, too.

"Hi there, Malinda. I didn't know you were back in Maplesville. You were somewhere in Texas, right?"

"Yep. Dallas. Moved there after Hurricane Katrina. My oldest just started at LSU so I decided to move back home. It was time."

Shayla nodded. "Eventually I guess we all come back home."

Malinda put a comforting hand on her shoulder. "I was so sorry to hear about Braylon," she said, her voice taking on that somber tone that usually accompanied any conversation surrounding Shayla's brother.

"Thank you. It hasn't been easy." She held up the coffee and pastries. "Where can I put these? Desiree usually delivers the goodies, but she's out sick."

"We have a break room back here. Thanks for providing the coffee, by the way," she called over her shoulder. "It means a lot."

"It's the very least I can do. The time you all volunteer at this place has been such a blessing for Gauthier's residents."

She followed Malinda into the break room and came face-to-face with the E.R. doctor from last night.

"Oh, great." Shayla snorted. She moved past him, setting the coffee and pastries on the square card table in the middle of the room. Then she turned around and addressed him. "Before that huge head of yours gets any bigger, know that I had no idea you would be here. This isn't some ploy to put me in your illustrious presence once again."

"I'm sorry about —"

She put both hands up. "I'm not interested in your apology."

"Is there a problem?" Malinda asked, looking back and forth between them.

"Oh, I just don't want God's gift to women over here thinking I'm going to attack him in a fit of passion."

He crossed his arms over his chest and slanted her a sardonic look. It goaded her that the egotistical bastard had the nerve to have such gorgeous eyes — eyes that were currently roaming over her with enough cynicism to choke a small animal.

"You done being self-righteous?" he asked.

"Not sure yet. Are you done accusing me of trying to commit child murder?"

Those striking eyes narrowed with irritation. "Don't you think you're blowing this out of proportion? And I apologize for what happened at the hospital last night."

"No, I don't think I'm blowing this out of proportion, and your apology is *not* accepted."

She brushed past him on her way out of the break room. He followed. So did Malinda, who seemed to be enjoying herself immensely, if the smile on her face was any indication.

"How is your niece doing?" he called after her.

"She's just fine. And if it'll put your mind at ease, know that I didn't try to poison her today."

She reached for the front door, but he stopped her, clamping a hand on her right shoulder. Shayla peered down at his hand, then looked up at him. "Remove it. Now," she ordered.

"Would you let me explain about last night?"

"Remove. It. Now."

He heaved a sigh and let go of her shoulder.

To Malinda, she said, "We need to catch up. Maybe we can have dinner? Or, better yet, come on over to The Jazzy Bean for lunch one day."

"Will do," Malinda said, amusement tracking across her face as she glanced over at Dr. Gorgeous Eyes.

Shayla refused to give him an ounce more of her attention. Without another word she turned and walked out the clinic's front door.

"So, you aren't married?"

"No, I'm not," Xavier answered. "Take a deep breath for me." He pressed the flat end of the stethoscope to Penelope Robottom's back.

"Divorced?"

"Nope. Another deep breath," he instructed.

Mrs. Robottom complied, but as soon as he removed the stethoscope, she continued on her fact-finding mission. "You have a girlfriend?"

"Mrs. Robottom, I don't think —"

"My daughter, Tabitha, is in the middle of a divorce right now. I never liked her husband. I would love for her to find someone sweet and successful, like you."

"Thank you for the compliment, but —"

She cut him off again. "Maybe the two of you can go out to dinner?"

Xavier's eyelids slid shut for a brief moment as he made notations on Mrs. Robottom's chart. He just didn't get it. Sure, he'd encountered his share of women whose eyes lit up at the sight of a white doctor's coat and no wedding ring, but this bordered on ridiculous.

How ironic that the only woman who had piqued his interest in the month since he'd come to Louisiana had looked as if she was ready to run him over with her car when she left after dropping off the coffee a few hours ago. Could he really blame her? After what he'd accused her of, he'd be lucky if Shayla Kirkland didn't report him to hospital administration.

He needed to smooth things over with her. Now that he knew she was the owner of the little coffee shop down the street, he at least knew where to find her.

"It sounds as if your lungs are clearing up nicely," Xavier told Mrs. Robottom. "But make sure you finish the round of antibiotics. Don't stop just because you're feeling better. If you notice any problems, come out to the hospital in Maplesville. Don't wait until we're back at the clinic here in Gauthier."

"I will, Dr. Wright. I'll see if Tabitha can bring me."

"Only come if there is a problem," Xavier reminded her. He had no doubt she'd be in the E.R. with her not-quite-divorced daughter by midweek.

He saw Mrs. Robottom to the lobby and turned the Open sign on the door to Closed once she and her husband, Nathan, had left the clinic.

"Good work today," Bruce said, coming up the hallway. He gestured to the lobby's collection of mismatched chairs. "How about a short debriefing? It shouldn't take more than ten minutes."

He, Malinda and Bruce, along with another RN and a nursing assistant, discussed the cases they'd seen that day. They all agreed that Gauthier was on the verge of a chicken pox outbreak. Four children under the age of twelve had been brought in with symptoms just that day.

Xavier was also concerned with the number of cases of diabetes. This was only his third week of volunteering at the clinic, which was opened three days a week for the residents of Gauthier, yet he'd seen at least a dozen cases of pre- and full-blown diabetes. In a town this size, that was reaching epidemic levels.

They discussed possibly extending the hours, or opening for a half day on Saturdays so that people who worked and couldn't make it to the clinic on a weekday could have access.

"Maybe we can start with every other Saturday to try it out," Malinda suggested.

"I'm up for that," Xavier said. It wasn't as if he had a social life getting in the way of his work. One of the pitfalls of working these temporary assignments was that it made establishing a life outside of work practically impossible.

Of course, that had been the number one reason he'd joined Good Doctors, Good Deeds, an organization that helped to staff hospitals in underserved communities by providing temporary physicians who agreed to work for significantly lower salaries. Money wasn't an issue for him — getting away from his hometown of Atlanta had been. Which was why he was on his third consecutive assignment with Good Doctors, Good Deeds.

"Okay, folks, that about does it," Bruce said. "Don't forget the barbecue at my place Friday. Xavier, you're off tomorrow, right?"

"Yep, then I switch to the graveyard shift."

"Don't worry," Malinda said. "It's the easiest of the three. Unlike in the big cities, things are quiet overnight around here."

"My last few assignments have been in rural communities. I'm just fine with the slower pace."

They all gave each other proverbial pats on the back for a job well done before closing down the clinic. Xavier followed Malinda into the employee break room and grabbed his backpack, then they both headed for the back door entrance that led to a small, graveled parking lot behind the clinic.

"Sooo," Malinda said, dragging out the word as she held the door open for him. "Those were some serious sparks of attraction I saw flying between you and Shayla today."

Xavier huffed out a laugh. "I'm not sure I'd call it that."

"Seemed pretty electric to me."

"I'm sure if she could have gotten away with it she would have scalded me with that hot coffee this morning." He unlocked his Jeep, but didn't get in. Leaning against the door, he stuffed his hands in the pockets of his green scrubs, and said, "She came into the E.R. last night with her niece, who'd gotten into the Easter egg dye."

"And?"

"And." Xavier scratched the back of his head. "Well, I may have accused her of purposely feeding the child the dye so that she would have a reason to take her to the E.R. And, you know, meet me."

A look of horror flashed across Malinda's face.

"I know. I know," Xavier said. "It's just that the women around here have gone to so many ridiculous lengths to visit my E.R."

He pointed to the clinic. "Just today Mrs. Robottom was hinting at hooking me up with her daughter, who is still married, by the way."

Malinda waved him off. "Tabitha and Lenny have been separated for longer than they've been married. It's about time they finally went through with the divorce. But Tabitha isn't right for you. You'd do better with someone without so much baggage. Shayla is actually perfect. She's single, the right age and successful in her own right."

"I'm not looking to get involved with anyone," Xavier said. "My assignment in Maplesville is for only three months. Between the hospital and volunteering at the clinic, I don't have time to catch the Braves games on TV, let alone date. That's not what I'm here for."

"I don't know how you do it." Malinda shook her head as she unlocked her car door. "It would drive me crazy moving from one hospital to another. You have to learn all new hospital politics, and you're always at the bottom of the totem pole." She stopped. "Oh, wait. You're an E.R. doctor. You're used to being at the bottom of the totem pole."

Xavier grinned at her good-natured barb, even though it stung way more than Malinda probably intended. The fact that he hadn't gone into one of the sexier specialties had triggered the beginning of the demise of his relationship with his ex-fiancée, Nicole. She'd found herself a cardiothoracic surgeon and quickly suckered him into putting a ring on her finger.

Xavier scrubbed his mind of the image of the wedding photo he'd seen in the society pages of the Atlanta newspaper, Nicole's orthodontics-enhanced smile staring back at him. He wasn't putting himself through that today.

"I hope your conflict with Shayla doesn't jeopardize our goodies," Malinda said through her open driver's-side window. "I'd hate to hurt your feelings when I choose coffee over you."

He chuckled. "I'd do the same if given the choice."

He tapped the roof of her car as she drove off.

Xavier set his backpack behind the seat and climbed into his Jeep Wrangler. As he came upon the intersection of Cooper Lane and Main Street, he spotted the sign for The Jazzy Bean about two blocks down. It featured a cartoon coffee bean playing a saxophone.

Ignoring the exhaustion that had him on

the verge of collapse, he pulled into an empty parking slot in front of Claudette's Beauty Parlor, locked the door — though it was hardly necessary in this small town — and a minute later walked through the front door of The Jazzy Bean.

The place was huge — much bigger than the average chain coffeehouse. Yet, despite its size, it still had a cozy feel. The polished concrete floors were stained a warm brown with hints of orange. A dozen small round table-and-chair sets occupied most of the space. A long, narrow bar lined with several stools ran the length of the floor-to-ceiling windows that faced Main Street.

Xavier stepped in a bit farther and noticed a stone-laid fireplace surrounded by several large wooden rocking chairs toward the rear of the coffeehouse. There was also a burnt-orange leather couch with two huge arm-chairs and a square ottoman. Several of the tables held chessboards, and a few had decks of cards. Framed black-and-white photographs of brass instruments, swamp-land scenes and coffee beans adorned brick walls. Despite the deep earth tones, the place was well lit with recessed lights and track lighting throughout.

"Nice," Xavier murmured. "Damn nice." It was much more than he'd expected to find in a small town like Gauthier.

He looked around, hoping to spot the person he'd come here for, but Shayla was nowhere to be found.

He walked over to a corkboard affixed to the wall, careful not to bump the table that had all the fixings for coffee — creamer, sugar, artificial sweeteners, honey and stirrers. Tacked to the corkboard were signs for various happenings in and around Gauthier. The civic association was sponsoring an Easter-egg hunt in Heritage Park. The local high school's 4-H Club was having a bake sale and car wash. There were Zumba classes right here at The Jazzy Bean on Tuesday and Thursday nights.

"Dr. Wright?"

Xavier turned. He pointed to the young lady who'd come into the E.R. over the weekend. "Erin, right?"

She nodded. "You remembered."

"Sure. How are you feeling?"

"Much better. You were right. It was just a stomach virus. Combined with the lack of sleep, it just wore me out."

"You mentioned the other day that you're premed. Sorry to break it to you, but the lack of sleep will only get worse."

She grimaced. "I've been told."

"Don't tell me you work here, too, in addition to going to school?"

"Only part-time," she said. "But that's about to change. I'm getting an apartment in New Orleans before the start of my next semester."

"And I will be very sorry to see her go."

Xavier turned to find Shayla sauntering up to them, her delicately flared hips swaying in a way that caused his skin to prickle with the same electricity that had jolted him last night in the E.R. Tied around her waist was an apron featuring the saxophone-playing coffee bean that was on the sign outside.

"Hello again," Xavier greeted.

"Hello," she said. Her tone lacked the sharpness that had colored it earlier today. That had to be a good sign, right?

She pointed at Erin. "You've got a paper due, which means you need to get out of here. Lucinda and I will close up."

Erin's relief was evident in her smile. "Thanks. I'll see you tomorrow."

Shayla turned back to him. "Sorry to kick you out, but we're closing in five minutes."

He pointed to the flyer tacked to the community board. "Says here that Zumba class starts at 6:30 p.m."

"You're here for Zumba?"

Her skeptical expression wrangled a laugh

out of him. "Maybe," Xavier answered.

"Hey, Shayla, would you tell this old woman to get me my apple fritter so I can leave?" They both turned at the sound of the gravelly voice calling from the counter.

"No fritters for you, Mr. Henry," Shayla said. "Imogen told me your cholesterol was up last week."

The older gentleman grunted and paid for the bran muffin.

"Sacrificing a sale for the well-being of your customer?" Xavier asked. "He could have just taken his business elsewhere."

"In case you haven't noticed, Doctor, when it comes to coffee and baked goods, I'm the only game in town. And I'm not willing to contribute to the rising health problems here in Gauthier just to make a few bucks."

"That's pretty noble of you."

"But not completely altruistic. The longer I can keep them alive, the longer I can have them as customers," she said, sending him a sassy wink. "I am a businesswoman, after all."

He laughed. "I need to adopt that motto. It works in my line of business, too." He followed her over to the tables and chairs and watched as she began wiping down the tabletops.

She looked up at him. "You're still here?"

He nodded. "And I will be until you accept my apology."

"Going to be a long, lonely night in this coffee shop for you. And if I find any inventory missing in the morning, I'm charging you for it."

"Why are you giving me such a hard time?"

"Because you accused me of jeopardizing my niece's health as a ploy to meet you. You'd better be grateful I haven't punched you in the gut. That was my first instinct."

"I am *begging* you to accept my apology for that. It was out of line, and I truly am sorry."

She spun around and planted the hand with the towel on her hip. "What could possibly make you jump to the conclusion that I was the one who'd given Kristi the dye?"

He held his hands out, pleading with her to understand. "Look, I've had an —" he tried to think of the right word "— an *interesting* introduction to this area. I seem to be very popular with the single ladies in Maplesville and Gauthier. I thought you were another one trying to sneak your way into my E.R."

"Oh, you don't have to tell me about your popularity," she said, moving to another table and resuming her task. "I happened to catch a gossip session yesterday that was all about the hot new doctor. I cannot believe how the women here are scheming just to get closer to you. It's ridiculous."

"Ouch," Xavier said after a pause. "Way to hurt my feelings."

She halted in the middle of wiping down the table, looked up at him and burst out laughing.

"That sounded awful, didn't it?" She shook her head. "I didn't mean that it was ridiculous that women would try to get closer to you. It's just the lengths they're going to that seem over the top. I'm sorry if I hurt your feelings, Dr. Wright."

The self-deprecating grin inching up the edges of her lips was as edible as any of the pastries in the display case. Xavier would bet it tasted better than any of them, too.

He leaned forward and whispered in her ear, "I'll accept your apology if you accept mine."

Her grin broadened. "Nice try."

The smile made her already gorgeous face even more alluring. For a moment, her full, gently bowed lips held him captive. She'd gathered her curly hair into a ponytail, making her regal cheekbones more pronounced.

"Shayla, I —"

He was cut off by a loud voice that yelled, "Auntie Shayla!"

The two little girls from last night ran out from a short hallway toward the rear of the coffeehouse.

"Auntie Shayla, is it almost time to dance?" the younger one asked. She looked no worse for wear after last night's E.R. visit.

When she spotted him, her eyes widened. "Dr. Wright!" She ran up to him, nearly crashing into his legs. "I'm not throwing up yellow stuff anymore."

"That's because he gave you medicine to make you feel better," the older girl said in that soft voice of hers.

"I'm happy it worked," Xavier said. "And we learned a lesson, right? No eating Easter egg dye, even if it is your favorite color?"

They both nodded.

"Dr. Wright is right," Shayla said, running a hand down each girl's head. "Dancing starts in a few minutes. Why don't you ask Ms. Lucinda to get you each some chocolate milk?"

"I want mine first," the youngest yelled as they both sprinted for the kitchen.

Shayla turned her attention back to him. "This has been fun, but in about ten minutes I'm going to have a bunch of women here looking to get their Zumba on, and I

61

need to have this place ready."

She started clearing the middle of the floor, dragging the chairs over to the wall. Xavier picked up a table and carried it over.

"Thanks, but you really don't have to do this."

"I know. It's all a part of my master plan to get in your good graces," he said with a wink. He got a glimpse of that grin again. Damn, but that grin was nice.

"So, there's a plan?" she asked.

Xavier nodded as he carted another table away. "Oh, yeah. I'm determined to get you to accept my apology."

She cocked her head to the side and stared at him for a moment.

"What?" Xavier asked.

She shook her head after another beat. "Nothing. Continue on. I'm usually doing this by myself, so it's nice to have some help."

He moved the last table, then walked up to her, stopping just inside of personal-space territory. "I'd be happy to come by in the evenings and help you move furniture around. Just let me know when to be here."

She didn't step back, which he took as a good sign. It meant that she was okay with him being in her personal space. A *very* good sign. He rather enjoyed her personal space.

The front door opened and two women walked in. Xavier recognized them as members of Gauthier's Civic Association. They stopped in at the clinic at least once a week to see if there was any help they could provide.

"Hey there, Mrs. Eloise and Mrs. Clementine," Shayla called. "Glad you two could make it." They both waved, but headed to the counter where the cook was packing up the leftover baked goods from the display case.

"That would be your cue to leave," Shayla said. "My class will be starting in just a few minutes."

"Have you accepted my apology yet?"

She pitched her head back and sighed dramatically at the ceiling. "Fine. I accept your apology."

"I'm not sure I believe you," Xavier said. "I think maybe I should apologize over dinner."

Her eyes widened in surprise. It seemed as if she was experiencing the same shock he was. Had he really just asked her out to dinner?

"You move pretty quickly, don't you?" Shayla asked.

No, he didn't. These days, when it came to women, he was the exact opposite of quick, especially after the way things had ended with Nicole. But now that he'd asked, he wasn't backing down. In fact, he was dying for her to say yes.

"I want to make up for last night's blunder." He reached for her hand. "Let me take you to dinner, Shayla."

When he touched her a current of electricity sparked between them. Xavier saw her breath catch. She stared down at their clasped hands, then back up at him. They stood there for several moments, the air between them crackling with a charged sizzle that he felt down to his toes.

Her eyes still locked with his, she slowly eased her fingers out of his grasp. "While I appreciate the invitation, I'm just too busy these days. I'm sorry, but I'll have to decline. Good night, Dr. Wright."

No way was he giving up this easily, not after the forceful surge that had overpowered the air between them a moment ago.

"What can I do to convince you to reconsider?" Xavier asked.

So now he was *pleading* for a date? What in the hell was going on with him?

A group of spandex-clad women of varying ages walked through the front door.

"Good night, Dr. Wright," Shayla said again.

Swallowing a frustrated groan, Xavier accepted defeat. For now.

"Good night," he said, staring at her retreating form as she turned and headed for one of the tables toward the back of the room. He continued to stare as she set up an iPod docking station and attached a set of speakers to it.

Just as he turned to leave, Margery Lambert, who'd brought her grandson to the clinic last week with a virus, stopped him. As she went on and on about the child's antics over the past week, the Zumba class started. Xavier barely registered Mrs. Lambert's words as Shayla began to instruct her students. His mouth dried up at the sight of her perfectly curved hips rotating to the Latin dance beats coming from the iPod.

God, she was beautiful. And sexy.

And definitely worth another attempt at asking out to dinner.

It took him a moment to reacquaint himself with the idea of actually pursuing a woman. Sure, he'd hooked up with a couple of women over the past year — women who knew from the start that he wanted a no-strings-attached deal. Dinner wasn't even expected, just a mutual meeting of body parts to fulfill a certain need. But when he'd asked Shayla to dinner, a casual hookup had been the last thing on his mind.

"Oh, I'm missing the warm-up," Mrs. Lambert said. "Anyway, Jayden is doing so much better. Thank you again, Dr. Wright. I am so grateful to have you and the others at the new clinic."

Xavier jerked to attention. Had she been talking to him this whole time?

"I . . . You're welcome," he said before Mrs. Lambert went over to join the rest of the class.

He lingered for a few minutes before forcing himself to exit the coffee shop. As he strolled to his Jeep, he prayed that visions of Shayla Kirkland's swaying hips didn't keep him up half the night.

"What about marshmallows?" Kristi clapped her hands excitedly and jumped up and down as if she'd just come up with the best recipe in the history of the universe.

"I'm not sure marshmallows will work in these cookies," Shayla said. "What if we try bulgur wheat, chai seeds and raisins?"

That got her the "you must be an alien who just sprouted two heads and an extra arm" look from both nieces.

"Okay, nix the chai," Shayla said. She'd

throw them in there when they weren't look-ing.

"And add chocolate chips," Kristi sug-gested.

They compromised on a dark chocolate drizzle. Even with the extra chocolate the cookies would still be better than the junk Shayla had encountered Kristi eating when she'd dropped in unannounced during snack time at school today. She'd walked into the classroom and had to stop herself from snatching the honeybun slathered with thick icing from her niece's hands.

Discovering what passed for snacks at Kristi's preschool only reaffirmed Shayla's quest to break the cycle of unhealthy eating habits in this area before her nieces fell into the trap. Tonight's baking adventure served double-duty. Not only was it another way to bond with the girls, but it also gave her a chance to test a few new recipes for The Jazzy Bean.

She'd been ecstatic to find a supplier in New Orleans that specialized in heart-healthy organic baked goods, but their prices had increased by 15 percent in the past six months. It was hard enough con-vincing customers to try the healthier op-tions; they definitely would not be willing to pay a premium for them.

"What time does mommy get here?" Kristi asked as she sprinkled in raisins a little at a time.

"She should be getting in any minute. Her airplane landed at eight o'clock."

Cass's eyes darted to the stove. "She's going to fuss at us for not being in bed."

"She'll be so happy to see you I think she'll forgive you this one time."

The sound of tires crunching the shelled driveway could be heard through the opened kitchen window.

"Mommy!" Cassidy and Kristi both screamed. They took off for the back door. Moments later, her sister-in-law walked into the house. She stooped and gathered her girls in a group hug.

"Welcome back," Shayla said, wiping dough from her fingers.

"It's good to be back," Leslie said. "I've missed you girls so much." She planted loud kisses on each daughter's cheek. "Did you two have fun with Auntie Shayla?"

Kristi nodded. "I went to the hospital."

Leslie's gaze flew to Shayla, her eyes wide with dismay. "What happened?"

Damn. She'd wanted to ease that bit of news into the conversation. She should have known Kristi would be eager to share her E.R. adventure with her mother.

"It turned out to be nothing," Shayla said.

"What's nothing?"

"Kristi ate the color that goes on the Easter eggs," Cassidy supplied.

Shayla quickly filled her in on yesterday's mishap.

"The E.R. visit was probably overboard, but I didn't want to take any chances," she tacked on.

After an awkwardly long silence that only ratcheted up Shayla's anxiety, Leslie smoothed a hand over Kristi's springy curls and said, "Well, I guess accidents happen."

Shayla's head snapped back in surprise. Of all the reactions that had swarmed through her head, that had *not* been one of them. She hadn't expected Leslie to yell and scream — that just wasn't in her sister-in-law's quiet nature — but she'd anticipated more of a reprimand, or at least a dirty look.

"You girls go and get your things," Leslie said. "It's past your bedtime and there's school tomorrow."

Shayla waited until they were alone before saying, "I really am sorry, Les."

"It's okay. I know how hard it is. You can't watch them every minute of every day."

"But I had to watch them for only a few days. I swear, I thought I would die when I saw Kristi vomiting all over the place."

69

"You should have been here when Cassidy got an ink pen cap stuck up her nose. Braylon needed more comforting than she did." Leslie laughed, then she covered her mouth with her hand as if she'd done something wrong.

Shayla's heart broke in two. "Oh, Leslie. There's nothing wrong with talking about him."

She took a step forward, intending to what? Hug her? Place a comforting hand on her shoulder?

It didn't matter, because Leslie backed away, moving to the counter where Shayla had stacked the DVDs, board games, and crayons and coloring books Leslie had provided before she'd left for Houston.

Tension suffused the air, the brief gaiety of a few moments ago obliterated by the mention of her brother's name.

If only she could figure out a way to get them all past their grief.

She was still learning her way when it came to her family, never sure how her gestures would be received. The truth of the matter was, she just didn't know them. And it was entirely her fault.

She'd received invitations to holiday gatherings, the girls' christenings, but she'd always had an excuse not to take that long flight back to Louisiana. Four times in nineteen years, that's how many times she'd returned home. She'd figured she'd have time for family later, once her brother was done with the army and his girls were older. Once she'd accomplished all those career goals that had come to rule her life.

Braylon's death had changed everything. It brought the importance of family into stark relief. Now that her brother was gone, Leslie and the girls were the only family she had left. She would figure out a way to connect with them. She refused to accept any other outcome.

The girls came running back into the kitchen carrying their overnight bags.

"Mommy, did you bring us back a present?" Kristi asked.

"Possibly," Leslie said. "You'll have to wait until we get home to find out."

"Do you need help getting them into the car?" Shayla asked.

"I think we're good. We're good, aren't we, girls?"

They both nodded.

Shayla followed them out to the car, anyway. Kristi kissed her on the cheek, but Cassidy only gave her a small wave before slipping into the backseat. Shayla continued to wave goodbye as Leslie backed the car out of the driveway. A minute later, Paxton's black Mazda hatchback pulled in.

"Were you waiting down the street?" Shayla asked when Paxton got out of the car.

"Yep." She held up a bottle of wine. "I figured you'd need this after your first extended weekend alone with your nieces."

Shayla enveloped her best friend in a hug, resting her cheek on her shoulder. "Do you see why I don't want you to leave? You always know just what to do."

Paxton patted her back. "Let's uncork this baby and make use of that lovely porch swing. Oh, wait!" She reached back into the car and came out with a second bottle of wine. "I heard about last night's visit to the E.R. I decided it called for an extra bottle."

"You'd better be happy I don't have a basement," Shayla told her. "I swear I'd lock you in there to prevent you from moving to Little Rock."

Paxton burst out laughing. "Come on. It's wine time."

As they sat on the porch swing enjoying the surprisingly humidity-free night air, Shayla filled Paxton in on her weekend with the girls. How some things had gone better than expected — like Kristi not crying for Leslie every night, which Shayla had fully anticipated. But how other things, particularly Cassidy's continued remoteness, remained the same.

"She's older," Paxton said. "It'll be more difficult for her to get over Braylon's death because she had more time with him."

"She probably overheard him talking about her selfish Aunt Shayla who never made any time for them. That's why she hates me."

"She doesn't hate you."

Shayla wasn't so sure about that. Cassidy was likely projecting the animosity her father had started to feel toward Shayla.

She'd loved her brother, and she knew he'd loved her. But she also knew that Braylon had become frustrated with her constant disregard of his many attempts to connect. He'd told her as much. He'd also threatened to cut her off completely if she didn't show more interest in being a part of his family.

"I did this to myself," Shayla said, taking another sip of pinot. "I have to live with it and just try harder with Cass. I'm taking them shopping for Easter dresses on Saturday. Maybe I can buy my way into Cassidy's good graces."

Shayla grimaced, setting her glass on the small glass-top table next to the swing. She didn't want to *buy* her niece's affections.

"You know, it may make a difference if you didn't spend so much time at The Jazzy Bean," Paxton said.

"What do you mean?"

"You moved back home to reconnect with your family, yet you're at the coffeehouse until after seven most nights. What does that give you, maybe an hour with the girls before their bedtime? What's the point of being back home if you're going to spend all your time working? You could have stayed in Seattle for that."

An uncomfortable feeling settled in Shayla's chest even as the proverbial light-bulb clicked on in her head. Paxton was right. She'd left her job back in Seattle, but she'd carried that workaholic attitude to Louisiana. How had she not recognized that she'd fallen into that same pattern?

"God, I am so stupid," Shayla said.

"Not stupid." Paxton rubbed her knee. "Just single-minded and determined. You've been that way your entire life. It's not a bad thing — look at what it did for your career."

"Well, I don't need to focus on my career anymore. I need to focus on making things work between me and Cassidy."

"You will," Paxton said. "But for now, I say we break into this second bottle. I'm leaving in a couple of days. We can wallow and cry and drink ourselves silly."

Shayla clinked her glass with the one her best friend held up to her. "Sounds like a plan."

CHAPTER 3

Xavier grabbed himself a bottle of water and settled on the couch. The minute he crossed his ankles on top of the worn chest that served as his coffee/dinner table, his cell phone rang.

Of course he'd left the phone over by the bed.

"Shit," he mumbled, pushing himself up from the couch.

He walked over to the queen-size bed that monopolized much of the studio he'd rented for his three-month stay in Maplesville. The apartment was built over a garage belonging to Dr. Mitchell Folse, the retired E.R. physician whose vacancy had created a need for Good Doctors, Good Deeds to send Xavier on this assignment. He could have booked a room at the extended-stay hotel in downtown Maplesville, but he'd grown tired of looking at the same kind of room in every city. At least this place had character, if not reliable hot water.

Besides, Mrs. Folse was a mastermind in the kitchen, and she always had a hot meal waiting for him when Xavier came home, no matter what time of the day or night he got in. Once a doctor's wife and all that.

He grabbed the phone from the nightstand and smiled at the number illuminating the screen.

"What's up, baby girl? How's it going in Hot-Lanta?"

"It's going just fine," his sister, Crystal, replied. "How's it going in Podunk, U.S.A.?"

"Maplesville, Louisiana," he corrected her.

"Doesn't matter. They're all Podunk, U.S.A., as far as I'm concerned."

"The wiseass never sleeps."

He reclaimed his spot on the couch and picked up the remote, powering up the forty-seven-inch flat-screen he'd gone out to buy the minute he'd spotted the fifteen-inch black-and-white Dr. Folse had in here.

"So, what's up?" he asked as he took a pull on his bottle of water and started flicking through channels.

He and his sister usually talked once a week, but their busy schedules had eaten into their chat time over the past few months. Crystal was finishing up her third year in endocrinology at Emory School of Medicine, continuing in the family legacy of physicians. His father was the only outlier. He was a research scientist.

Once he got the scoop on her workload, Xavier and Crystal spent the next ten minutes discussing her newest hobby: sky-diving.

"I can only imagine what Mom has to say about that one," Xavier said.

"I got that vein in her forehead to make an appearance. You know that hasn't happened since you wrecked the house with that party you threw back in high school. Oh, and speaking of houses, you would not believe who I just heard is losing theirs."

His sister went on to regale him with the latest juicy scandals to hit Buckhead, the affluent Atlanta suburb where he grew up. Xavier couldn't care less about which wealthy socialite had squandered their money away, but that didn't stop Crystal from sharing. His sister lived for that stuff.

Maybe if he hadn't been the subject of such gossip not too long ago . . .

"Okay, enough about that," Crystal said after another five-minute soliloquy on the number of neighbors who'd had plastic surgery this month. "How are they treating you at this latest hospital?"

Despite the teasing he knew would follow, he told her about his status as Maplesville's hot new item. When he recounted the incident with Shayla, and the way she'd laid into him the next day, Crystal laughed so hard Xavier was sure she'd need to be resuscitated.

"You just about done?" he drawled as he settled on a basketball game.

"Not yet." He waited while she continued to laugh at his expense. "I'm trying to feel sorry for you, but it sounds as if you deserved that ass-chewing."

"Yeah, I deserved it."

"Besides getting your butt handed to you, which I am *so* sorry I missed, by the way, how is everything else going?"

He told her about the clinic and how she could probably do a case study on the concentration of patients with diabetes he'd come across in his first month of volunteering.

"But don't worry, I'm not asking you to move here. I know you wouldn't be caught dead in a town this small," Xavier said. "You used to cry to go back to Atlanta after just a day at Gram and Pop's house."

"I'm a city girl. I make no apologies," his sister said.

"You just don't want to miss out on any

of that juicy city gossip," Xavier teased.

"Speaking of gossip . . ." She hesitated for a moment, before saying, "News around the hospital is that Nicole and Steven are pregnant."

His entire body grew taut at her pronouncement.

Xavier willed himself not to have any reaction whatsoever to the news that his ex-fiancée and her new husband were expecting a baby, but damn, how could he not? Especially when one of the biggest bones of contention between them was Nicole's adamant insistence that she didn't want children. That and her disgust over Xavier "settling" for a life in the E.R. instead of a more prestigious specialty.

"I'm sorry," Crystal said. "I know this isn't something you wanted to hear, especially today."

Xavier blew out a tired breath as he reclined, letting his head rest on the back of the sofa.

"Why should today make any difference?" he asked, staring unseeingly at the ceiling's unpainted wooden slats.

"Well, it's the fourth," Crystal answered.

It took a moment for her words to register.

April 4th. If he and Nicole had stayed together, this would have been their first anniversary.

"Wow." Xavier ran a hand down his face. "Today's date slipped right past my radar."

"Oh, great," Crystal said. "And here I am reminding you. I'm so sorry, Xavier."

"Don't worry about it," he said. "She's having a baby. Good for her. I hope it spits up on every one of her designer dresses."

Crystal barked out a sharp laugh, but he didn't join her. He cringed at his petty bitterness. He was better than this, although it didn't feel that way right now. Right now, he wanted to sulk and think bad thoughts about the woman who'd broken his heart.

"I won't lie," his sister said. "When I heard about it, the first thing I thought was that that should have been *my* niece or nephew. It's amazing how quickly things change, huh?"

The disappointment in his sister's voice caused a knot of pain to tighten in his gut. He wasn't the only one affected by his broken engagement. His entire family had fallen in love with Nicole. Too bad she hadn't reciprocated that love.

"I hate to end the convo on this sucky note," Crystal said. "But I'm meeting Amanda for a movie in a half hour. I'll talk to you later this week, okay?"

"Yeah, okay," Xavier said. "Give Mom and

Dad a kiss from me."

"Will do. Love you, sweetie."

"Love you."

He ended the call and tossed the phone on the sofa next to him. Covering his face with both hands, Xavier pitched his head back and sucked in a deep breath.

A baby.

The woman he was supposed to marry was having a baby with another man. Just how in the hell was he supposed to take that news?

He couldn't be happy for her. Not yet. That was asking way more of him than he could give.

He needed to be indifferent, but Xavier found that he couldn't do that either, especially after being reminded of today's date. Now all he could think about was how different today would have been if he and Nicole were still together, celebrating their anniversary, possibly sharing the happy news of their own baby with family and friends.

If only he had —

"Oh, hell no," Xavier said.

He'd given up playing the *if only* game a long time ago.

If only he had gone into another specialty. *If only* he had spent more time with her. *If only* he had given her the moon, and the stars and everything else in the damn sky.

It still wouldn't have been enough.

He could have given Nicole everything, and he would still be in this very same place, doing this very same thing. Because the problem wasn't with him. It never had been. The problem was with her. No matter how hard he'd tried, nothing he did could ever make her happy.

"You're not putting yourself through this shit today," Xavier muttered. He pushed up from the sofa and stalked over to the battered chest of drawers.

He'd planned to skip Bruce's get-together, wanting to do nothing but rest after working the overnight shift two nights in a row. But there was no way in hell he was sitting around this tiny apartment all day thinking about his ex-fiancée and her impending bundle of joy. The *what could have been*'s were sure to drive him crazy.

Pulling out a pair of worn jeans and his favorite Meharry Medical T-shirt, Xavier quickly dressed for the barbecue. As he looked around the studio apartment, he was struck with a feeling of discontent unlike any he'd experienced in a long time. He was tired of going from one bland hotel room to another. He was tired of not being able to plan anything longer than a couple of months in advance because he wasn't sure where his next assignment would have him living.

Dammit. He should have let Crystal's call go to voice mail. His mood had taken a one-eighty since he'd talked to her.

He unhooked his keys from the single thick nail next to the door and bounded down the outside stairs.

By the time he arrived at Bruce's there were a half-dozen cars parked in front of the two-story brick home. Bruce waved him over to where several doctors from the hospital were sitting under the canopy of a pecan tree. There was a television set up on a wooden picnic table, the basketball game he'd been watching at home on the screen.

He accepted the beer Bruce handed him and sat back in the lone available reclining lounge chair.

"What have I missed?" Xavier asked.

Bruce pointed to a tree house in the large oak on the opposite side of the yard. "David's twins got in a knock-down, drag-out fight with a mother bird after they messed with her nest over there," he said. "The twins lost. Both got pecked on the head."

"It was hard as hell not to laugh while I patched them up," David McHenry, who

84

ran the pediatric department at Maplesville General, said.

"I guess being a pediatrician comes in handy," Xavier said.

"More often than you would imagine. I think we can all attest to that," he said, garnering laughs from the rest of the men.

Xavier had hoped coming here would improve his mood, but as his colleagues told stories of how they'd all called on David after antics their kids had pulled, he was staggered by the sense of longing that suddenly overwhelmed him. He'd always wanted children, but after Nicole had decided she didn't, he'd willingly given up on that dream.

And look what he'd gotten in return for his sacrifice. He'd spent the past year living like a nomad, going from one place to another, while Nicole had been living the life *he* wanted — a life she'd claimed she wasn't interested in.

Xavier took in Bruce's backyard: the tree house, the wooden swing set, the basketball hoop.

This is what he wanted.

He wanted the picket fence. He wanted a marriage like his parents and grandparents had, the kind that made people stop and stare because their unabashed love was so apparent. He wanted kids who would drive him crazy, but also give him something to come home to.

Unbidden, Shayla Kirkland's stunning face popped to the forefront of his mind.

What in the heck was it about her?

He knew the women who washed clothes at the Maplesville Laundromat on Wednesday mornings better than he knew her. Yet, there she was, front and center, filling his mind with inappropriate thoughts disguised as Zumba moves.

Maybe he should have just stayed at home and thought about Shayla dancing Zumba all day. Sans clothing. Now *that* was an image that was certain to get him in trouble. But, dear God, it was a nice thought.

David's twins ran up to him, both climbing onto their father's lap. And just like that, thoughts of what he'd been missing — of what Nicole would soon have with her new husband and new baby — came roaring back.

Xavier gripped the plastic handles of the lounge chair and lunged up.

"Hey, Bruce, where's the washroom?" he asked.

Bruce pointed to the small building a few yards from the house. "Use the one in my almost-finished man cave. Give me a few more weekends and we'll be watching the game in there instead of under this tree."

Xavier walked over to the structure, which was empty save for a few sheets of drywall and a couple gallons of paint. The tiny bathroom was functional, though. He closed the door and leaned his head back, closing his eyes against the rush of emotion that damn near brought him to his knees.

He wasn't up for dealing with this. Not here. Not today.

Why was he questioning these things now? He liked the life he'd carved out for himself. Working with Good Doctors, Good Deeds suited him to perfection. He swooped in. Did his job. Then moved on. It was the very definition of *bliss*. At least that's what he'd been telling himself for the past year.

But given just a small window to examine it and Xavier saw things for exactly what they were. He was running. He'd been running since the day Nicole had handed him her engagement ring.

He'd put his dreams aside for her, but it was time he finally accept that she was no longer a part of his life. And she never would be.

Xavier knew the time was coming soon when he would have to take a long, hard look at his life and decide what he wanted out of it. He couldn't continue this way.

He'd spent the past year existing. It was time he started *living* again.

"What about this one?"

Shayla looked up from the spinning rack of lace-laden dresses, one of at least three dozen in Carly's Closet, which claimed to have the largest selection of Easter dresses in southeast Louisiana. It was the fifth store they'd visited this morning at the ridiculously huge outlet mall in Maplesville.

"I like it," Shayla said of the dress Leslie held up. She motioned to her shoulders. "I'm just not sure about the huge bows on the arms. That would drive me crazy. What do you think, Cass?"

Her niece eyed the dress with a glare that told Shayla better than words exactly what she thought about it. Leslie looked at her daughter and blew out an irritated breath.

"Fine," Leslie said. "We'll find something else. Goodness, if she's this picky now I don't want to think about the teenage years."

Shayla laughed, sympathizing with her sister-in-law. She'd found herself laughing a lot this morning; they all had. Even Cassidy had given her a grin when Shayla had teased Kristi with a dress that had ugly, bug-eyed frogs stitched around the hem.

It felt . . . nice. Normal. Like an ordinary outing that most families engaged in without giving it a second thought.

If only this could become the norm. Shayla was afraid to let herself hope, but just the thought caused a flutter of optimism to lift her stomach.

They'd driven over early this morning, wanting to get here before the crowds, and had spent the past couple of hours laughing, shopping and just having a good time. She'd been surprised by Leslie's candidness. Her sister-in-law was still so reserved with her. But this morning Leslie had shared stories from last weekend's wedding, and the fun she and her female cousins had had in Houston.

Other than Paxton, Shayla hadn't had many girlfriends. This morning had showed her what she had been missing. How awesome would it be if she and Leslie could get past the awkwardness between them and be *real* sisters?

"What about this one?" Shayla asked, holding up a gorgeous pale green dress with white lace trim and hand-stitched smocking at the waist.

"It's sleeveless," Cassidy said.

"Well, what's wrong with that? Most of

the dresses are sleeveless because it's so hot this time of year."

"Cass doesn't do sleeveless," Leslie said. She came around the rack and held the dress at the hem, spreading it out. "Although, this is a very pretty dress, Cassidy. Maybe we can find a light sweater for you to wear with it?"

"But what's wrong with sleeve — ?" Shayla started, but a loud crash snagged her attention.

They all looked over to find the display case with pastel hair ribbons in pieces, scattered on the floor. Kristi stood next to it, her hand covering her mouth.

"I wanted the bunny," she said. She pointed to the floppy-eared bunny that had been part of the store's Easter decorations.

Shayla hung the dress back on the spinner rack. "Let's get out of here before we get tossed out."

"Good thinking," Leslie said, ushering Kristi and Cass out. "Anybody hungry?"

Several minutes later they lucked out, scoring a recently vacated table in the busy food court. After taking orders, Shayla left Leslie with the girls while she walked up to the pretzel-and-hot-dog place and put in their order.

A deep voice from just over her shoulder

said, "Get the one with jalapeño and cheese. It's the best."

Shayla spun around, finding Xavier Wright mere inches from her. She put a hand to her heart, which, not surprisingly, had started beating like a tambourine just at the sight of him.

"Are you trying to drum up business for the E.R., Dr. Wright?"

"Not really." He laughed. "Especially with it being my day off. But if you're going to have a coronary, aren't you happy I'm around?"

"I'd be happier if you didn't *cause* the coronary."

With that panty-dropping smile he produced so effortlessly he leaned over and, in a silken whisper, said, "I've seen you Zumba. I think your heart can take it. Now, whether or not mine can is a different story. I've been having a hard time getting that picture of your hips shaking out of my head."

Those words, delivered in that rich, honeyed voice, caused a spark to ignite in her blood, setting off a chain reaction that had inappropriate thoughts bombarding her. That was not a good thing, especially with her nieces just a few yards away.

She took a couple of steps back, putting

91

some much-needed distance between them. Not as if it helped with controlling her body's response to him. Her skin pebbled with attraction-induced goose bumps.

"This is the last place I expected to find you," Shayla said, taking yet another step back. She didn't want to give temptation a fighting chance. She gestured to his jeans and faded T-shirt. "You don't come across as a clotheshorse."

He shrugged. "A buddy of mine is coming to New Orleans and invited me to dinner at a restaurant that doesn't allow jeans. That's the only reason I'm here. I'd rather eat nails than spend time in a mall." He nodded toward the table where Leslie and the girls sat. "You all getting in some last-minute Easter shopping?"

"Yeah. It's been an exhausting morning." She looked back at the table and caught Kristi waving her hand like a maniac. Shayla chuckled. "My youngest niece has the biggest crush on you ever since her visit to the E.R."

"What about her aunt?" Xavier asked, his voice dropping several octaves. "Does she have a crush on me, too?"

That silken voice triggered another physical response from her body, in a place that had no business responding in the middle of a crowded food court.

"Kristi's aunt is a bit too old for crushes," Shayla answered, hoping her face didn't look as flushed as it felt.

He shook his head. "I'm living proof that you're never too old for a crush. I've got a pretty big one on a certain coffee shop owner."

Oh, yeah, her face was definitely flushed.

"Are you trying to see how much you can make me blush?" she asked.

"I'm trying to see if I can convince you to have dinner with me."

The teen working behind the counter called Shayla's number and pushed a tray loaded with hot dogs and thick, Belgian pretzels toward her. She reached for the tray but Xavier scooped it up before she had a chance.

He held the tray up, his eyes scanning the contents. "I thought you were the health food czar?"

"*Czar* is a bit too dictator-ish," she said. "I prefer health food crusader."

"So hot dogs and pretzels aren't evil?"

"Nothing is evil in moderation." She reached for the tray, but he moved it out of her reach. Shayla put her hands on her hips. "You're not planning to hold our food hostage until I accept your dinner invitation, are you?"

"Actually, I just thought I'd be a gentleman and carry it to the table, but now that you mention it, holding your food hostage isn't such a bad idea."

Her eyes narrowed with reproach.

"Fine," he said. "But I still want you to accept my dinner invitation. I want that so damn much, Shayla," he said, his voice turning sincere. "We got off to a rough start. Let me make it up to you."

She stared at him for several moments, everything within her screaming at her to say yes. But then she looked back at the table where Leslie, Cassidy and Kristi were all staring with wide-eyed fascination. The hero worship on Kristi's face sealed the deal for her.

"I can't," Shayla said. She shook her head. "There's just . . . My focus should be on the girls. Between them and my business, I just can't."

Before he had the chance to speak she snatched the tray from his hands. Her limbs were trembling so badly that soda dribbled from the cups as she carried the tray.

"Well, that was interesting," Leslie said when Shayla arrived back at the table.

She released the breath she'd been holding since leaving Xavier at the food counter.

"That was . . . I don't know what that was,"
Shayla said. She dispensed the food and
executed a quick subject change before Leslie could ask any questions she didn't have
answers to. "So, Cass, did you tell your
mom about softball?" Shayla asked.

"Softball?" Leslie's brows arched.

Panic shone in Cassidy's eyes as her gaze
darted from Shayla to Leslie.

"Uh-oh," Shayla said, sensing she'd
messed up. "Was it a secret?"

"That can't be, because Cassidy knows
that we don't keep secrets," Leslie said.

Cassidy's distress was palpable as she
reached into the American Girl jean purse
that she was never without and came up
with a wrinkled sheet of paper.

"They gave us letters on Monday," she
said, handing the form to Leslie.

Leslie's eyes roamed over the note. "Cass,
I don't know about this. You already have
Bayou Campers."

"But softball practice will be only two days
a week. And practice will last only one hour.
And you don't have to worry about money
because Mrs. Brown said all the uniforms
and equipment are being donated. And
games are on Saturday mornings only."

Shayla had to close her mouth. It had
fallen wide-open listening to Cassidy's plea.

It was the most she'd ever heard her niece speak at one time.

Leslie set the paper on the table. "And I have a job, and I have to take care of you and your sister, and I have to clean up after you when you forget to pick up your art supplies. There are only so many hours in the day, Cass. You can't do everything."

The disappointment that instantly washed over Cassidy's face made Shayla's heart lurch.

"I can do it," she said.

What?

"You can?" Leslie asked.

No, she couldn't. Not even a little. Not at all.

She didn't know the first thing about softball. The last time she'd played was in her sophomore P.E. class. Romy Chesterfield had purposely dinged her with the ball, giving Shayla a knot on her hip that didn't go down for two weeks.

But when she looked at her niece all she could see was a little girl who was the spitting image of her brother, and who, at present, had eyes full of doubt, as if she didn't trust Shayla to really mean what she'd just promised. She was not letting Cassidy down again.

"Yes," Shayla said. "It can't be that hard, can it?"

"But you have a business to run," Leslie pointed out.

"I can bring my laptop and catch up on paperwork while Cass and her team practices."

"Bringing her to practice is only one part of it," Leslie said. "This new position I just accepted has me so busy at work, I can't promise that I'll be able to do half the things that'll be expected of parents."

"What sort of things?" Shayla asked, unable to mask the trepidation in her voice.

"Things like helping out in the concession booth, collecting tickets at the gate, and whatever else they can come up with. It's not as simple as sitting through a couple of softball practices and games on Saturday morning."

Her first instinct was to tell Leslie "Yes, you're right," and back out of the deal, but she'd said she would do it, and she would not allow herself to backpedal. *This* was why she'd come back home. *This* was what was important to her.

She had been struggling to find a way to connect with Cassidy. All of her attempts thus far had yielded nothing but the same shy, standoffish looks from her niece. Shayla looked at her now and saw something that made her heart lurch in an entirely new, intoxicating way.

She saw affection. And admiration.

"Please," Shayla said to Leslie. "I want to do this. I *need* to do this."

"Please, Mom," Cassidy's soft voice pleaded.

Leslie looked back and forth between them before finally relenting. "Fine. This is between you and your aunt Shayla. If she agrees to do it, it's fine with me."

"Yes!" Cassidy bounded out of her seat, ran over to Shayla and hugged her. "Thank you, Aunt Shayla."

Feeling her niece's arms wrapped around her brought on euphoria unlike any Shayla had ever experienced. Her throat squeezed tight with emotion, to the point that she could barely swallow.

"Thanks for letting me, sweetheart," she managed to choke out.

She may not know the first thing about softball, but if it meant building a relationship with Cassidy she would happily endure hours of softball practice. She was afraid to get her hopes up too high, but she couldn't help but think that she'd finally found a way to accomplish the one thing that had thwarted her since she'd moved back to

Gauthier. She'd finally found a way to connect with her niece.

CHAPTER 4

Shayla packed a dozen of her newest heart-healthy creation — a date, candied ginger and agave-nectar breakfast bar — into a bakery box, along with a couple of chocolate chip scones for those who didn't care about their waistlines or arteries. She set the pastries next to the gallon of coffee for the clinic, and then filled a paper bag with napkins, raw-sugar packets and coffee stir-rers.

The door chime preceded Mariska Thomas as she entered The Jazzy Bean. The hairstylist didn't miss a morning of coming in for a double-shot latte and blueberry muffin before starting her workday at Claudette's Beauty Parlor, just a few storefronts down on Main Street.

"Morning, Mariska," Shayla greeted. "Give me a minute and I'll be right with you."

"No, she won't," Erin said as she backed

out of the swinging kitchen door, carrying a tray of croissants. She slid the tray inside the display case, and then took her usual place behind the counter. She hooked a thumb at Shayla. "Whenever she tries to wait on you, just ignore her. She has a hard time understanding that she has employees for a reason."

Shayla rolled her eyes.

Mariska laughed. "Uh-oh, sounds as if you're being pushed out, Shayla."

"I've been forbidden to wait on customers in my own coffee shop."

"It's for your own good," Desiree called as she came around the counter. She picked up the plate Lucinda had just placed in the window. "Now, are you sure you don't want me to deliver the coffee to the health clinic?"

"No, I can at least do that," Shayla said. "Besides, I need to speak with one of the doctors there."

"I'll bet I know which one," Mariska said. "Is it that fine Dr. Wright?"

Lucinda poked her head through the cutout window. "He's come in here at least five times in the last two days sniffing after this one."

Shayla swung around. "Sniffing after? What am I, a dog?"

"Don't try changing the subject."

Shayla's cheeks started to heat as three sets of eyes drilled her with knowing looks.

"Oh, for crying out loud! Yes, it's Dr. Wright," she admitted. "But his being fine has nothing to do with why I need to speak with him."

"I don't know why not," Lucinda huffed. "I'm ready to go cougar on him my damn self."

Erin choked out a laugh. "Go cougar on him?"

"Girl, yes. That's the new thing, you know?" Lucinda looked around before saying in a loud whisper, "You'd never believe who Margery Lambert is with."

Shayla put a hand up. "I don't even want to know." Some visual images were better left unimagined, and Margery Lambert "with" *anyone* was one of them.

She would have to keep her eye on Lucinda. She could totally see her "accidentally" cutting herself with a paring knife in hopes of scoring a trip to the E.R. to "go cougar" on Xavier.

Just as she reached for the coffee and pastries, Shayla heard an earsplitting grinding noise, followed by a loud pop and Erin's "Holy crap!"

A thick stream of smoke bellowed from the top of her extremely expensive commercial espresso machine.

Shayla rushed behind the counter. "Are you okay?" she asked Erin, who stood wide-eyed, her hand over her heart.

"Yeah, I'm good," Erin said. "A little freaked out, but good."

Desiree rushed back from where she'd just delivered Harold Porter's omelet and wheat toast. "What happened here?"

"It sounded like the grinder to me," Erin said.

"We just had this machine serviced a couple of weeks ago."

"How much do you want to bet the service guy knocked something out of place?" Lucinda said.

"Or didn't properly clean out the gears," Erin added.

Shayla heaved a sigh toward the ceiling. "I'll call the service company."

"You'll deliver coffee to the health clinic," Desiree said.

"That can wait," she said. "Contacting the service company is more important."

"I know it is. You want to know something else? It's my job."

"It's my coffee shop," Shayla reminded her.

Desiree crossed her arms over her chest and gave her a severe look. "You do realize that I get paid the same amount whether you do my job or I do it, right? You'd just as well let me earn my paycheck."

Shayla's first instinct was to tell her it didn't matter; it was her espresso machine and she was going to handle it. Loosening the reins and learning to trust others to do their jobs had been, by far, the hardest thing she'd had to do since opening The Jazzy Bean. This coffee shop was her livelihood. She'd invested a huge chunk of her nest egg into it; how could she *not* be involved in every aspect of the business?

But Desiree had a point. Shayla had hired a manager so that she wouldn't be bogged down in the day-to-day operation of The Jazzy Bean. In fact, in the beginning, she was only supposed to drop in occasionally. But she'd gradually found herself spending more and more time at the coffeehouse and having to squeeze time into her day to see the girls.

Paxton's earlier observation resurfaced. What was the point of moving to Gauthier if she remained the workaholic she'd been back in Seattle?

Goodness! Would she ever learn?

"You're right," she told Desiree. "You handle the espresso machine." She pointed at her. "But if that repair company gives you a hard time you tell me."

"I'm capable of giving as good as I get, but I'll keep you up-to-date. Now get over to that clinic. There's a fine single doctor who makes no bones about how much he's interested in you. With all the women who've crashed and burned seeking his attention, I may just have to smack you if you let this opportunity pass you by."

"Yeah, Shayla." Mariska nudged her. "You need to get it on with Dr. Hottie. Do it for all of us."

Shayla bit her bottom lip to stop herself from laughing. She grabbed the coffee and pastries again, and as she was backing out of the front door, said, "I'll be back before the lunch rush. Remember to call me if you need me, Desiree."

"I won't," her manager answered. She laughed as Desiree stuck her tongue out at her just as the door swung closed.

Shayla would be the first to admit that she was never good at being a team player, especially when there was so much riding on the outcome. She'd been burned too many times in her former job, putting her heart and soul into a team project, only to have it usurped by a ruthless coworker. Or worse, having to share the blame when someone on the team messed up. She'd rather just do the job herself and make sure it was done right.

But she'd hired three excellent women to staff her coffeehouse. She could trust them to hold things together at The Jazzy Bean. She had other things she could devote her time and energy to. One of those things had prompted this visit to see a certain E.R. physician this morning.

As she walked along the brick-paved sidewalk, Shayla tried to ignore the uptick in her pulse and the fact that the tingling along her skin increased with every step that brought her closer to the clinic on Cooper Lane.

Tingling skin? A rapidly beating heart?

Goodness, was she thirty-six, or sixteen?

Her birth certificate said one thing, but over the past week and a half she'd felt more like a teenager with a massive crush than a seasoned businesswoman who'd spent the past dozen years holding her own in corporate America.

Of course, Xavier didn't give her much choice *but* to think about him, since he seemed to be everywhere.

Monday, while serving sandwiches to a couple who'd opted to eat at one of the coffeehouse's outside tables, she'd glanced across the street and noticed him coming out of the Gauthier Pharmacy and Feed Store. He'd waved and smiled, and she'd spent the next ten minutes trying to control the stupid grin that refused to leave her face.

When he'd come over for coffee Tuesday morning, he'd invited her to a movie at the new megascreen multiplex that had recently opened in Maplesville. Shayla had been shocked at how quickly she'd almost accepted, but then she remembered that she'd promised to help Kristi with her school project, making an Easter bunny out of cotton balls and paper plates.

Yesterday, Xavier had stopped in at The Jazzy Bean for breakfast, and once again her heart rate had skyrocketed to ridiculous levels and stayed there for the duration of his visit. He'd come back at lunch, and then again around closing time. It wasn't until after he'd left for the third time that Shayla remembered that the clinic wasn't open on Wednesdays, which meant he'd driven all the way from Maplesville *three* times in one day just to eat at her coffeehouse.

Well, and to shamelessly flirt.

He didn't even try to be subtle about it. He'd turned down Erin's attempt to take his order, opting to wait a full ten minutes until Shayla was free and could wait on him. When she finally did, he asked her to dinner. Every single time.

A part of her wished he really was the arrogant jerk she'd pegged him to be when she'd brought Kristi into the E.R. Maybe if she knew he was a jerk her body wouldn't react the way it did at just the thought of him.

But he wasn't conceited or egotistical or any of the other things she'd accused him of being. And after hearing the way some of the women who came into The Jazzy Bean talked about him, Shayla couldn't blame him for being suspicious of the motives of every woman who stepped into his E.R.

As she approached the clinic, the front door opened and Matthew Gauthier walked out.

"Hey there, Matt," Shayla called.

"Shayla! Hi." Ever the gentleman, he quickly made his way down the steps and took the coffee and pastries from her hands. "Fate must realize that I'm behind schedule today," he said. "The Jazzy Bean was my next stop."

"If you head there right now you can beat the lunch crowd," she said over her shoulder as she climbed the porch steps ahead of him.

"I wish I was going for food. Tamryn's been packing my lunch." His grimace imparted exactly how he felt about his fiancée's cooking. "I wanted to talk to you about providing the refreshments for a special meet and greet I'm hosting for residents of District Twelve."

"Keeping that campaign pledge you made, huh?" Shayla held the door open for him, then gestured for him to follow her to the small employee break room where Malinda had guided her the last time she'd delivered coffee and treats.

"I promised to give constituents an outlet to voice their concerns." He set the coffee and pastries on the counter and turned to her. "I'm hoping I can do it once a quarter, or even more, depending on the needs of the community."

"Gauthier is lucky to have you as a voice, Matt."

His humble smile was so like him. She'd always liked Matthew Gauthier. His family had founded the town, but he never put on airs.

"So, does this sound like something you can handle?" he asked.

"Sure. Would you require someone there to serve the food, or can I just see that the items are delivered?"

"I'll swing by and pick the stuff up myself if I have to. I just want a good turnout, and I figure free food is a surefire way to get people in the door."

"That usually does it." Shayla laughed. "The Jazzy Bean hasn't done a catering job before, but there's a first for everything. Stop by later and we can hash out the details."

"Sounds good. Thanks a lot, Shayla."

Tingles skittered across her skin seconds before a voice from just over her shoulder said, "I thought you'd already left?"

"I had, but I got lured back in by a pretty lady carrying coffee." Matt stopped on his way out of the break room and kissed her cheek. "Thanks again. I'll be in touch."

Shayla sucked in a fortifying breath before turning to find Xavier leaning casually against the doorjamb.

Why did he have to wear that white coat and those green scrubs so damn well?

His mouth held the barest hint of a smile, but there was no denying the pleasure sparkling in his deep brown eyes. Just the suggestion that the look in his eyes had anything to do with her had Shayla's heart rate suddenly trying to compete with the speed of light.

Calm the heck down, she mentally chastised, but her body's response to him was the direct opposite of calm. She couldn't remember the last time she'd been so affected by a man's mere presence.

With amusement tinting his deep voice, he said, "I know you think my ego is already bigger than Jupiter, but I happen to know for a fact that the young lady who usually delivers the coffee is back at work. So, I can only conclude that you chose to deliver it this morning because you want to see me."

She made a tsking sound and shook her head. "Your poor neck must be exhausted."

He brought a hand to the back of his neck and rubbed, his forehead furrowed in confusion. "Why's that?"

"Having to carry around that massive head of yours."

He dropped his hand and slayed her with another of those devastating grins. Her heart skipped another beat. It needed to stop doing that.

"You don't pull any punches do you?" Maintaining that relaxed pose, he crossed his arms over his chest. "It's a good thing I have a healthy self-esteem."

"As if I could wound your pride."

"I'm more sensitive than you think."

Shayla rolled her eyes. With the number of women constantly throwing themselves at him, she had no doubt his self-confidence was very much intact.

"It's not as if you need the ego stroke, but

it just so happens that I *am* here to see you."

His eyebrows lifted in genuine surprise.

"Do tell," he said. He pushed away from the doorjamb and joined her in the break room. Grabbing a plain white mug from the counter, he filled it with coffee from the traveler box. He sipped and let out a satisfied sigh. "God, you brew a good cup of coffee."

She cursed the streak of giddiness that coasted along her skin.

"Thank you," Shayla said. She had no business letting his simple compliment affect her this much. Heck, she hadn't even brewed this morning's coffee. If anyone should feel giddy, it was Erin.

"So, are you here to finally accept my apology, or my invitation to dinner, or both?" he asked.

"I thought I already accepted your apology?"

"Your acceptance wasn't sincere enough for me to believe that you really meant it."

Her brow pinched. "There are degrees of acceptance?"

"Of course. And on a scale of one to ten, your acceptance was a three." He squinted and wiggled his hand. "Maybe a three-and-a-half."

He took a couple of steps forward, his

whiskey-brown eyes focused on her. "Now that I have you on my turf, I can do this properly." He took both of her hands and held them between his palms. Awareness prickled where he touched her. "I need you to know how profoundly sorry I am for accusing you of harming your niece. It was unprofessional and unfair, and if I could take it back I would."

For a moment, Shayla was struck speechless, entranced by the depth of his gaze and the enticing cadence of his rich voice.

"I . . . I understand." She slowly slid her fingers out of his hold. She couldn't concentrate with him touching her. She took a couple of steps back and rubbed her hands up and down her arms, which were suddenly covered with goose bumps.

"Do you really, Shayla?"

"I do," she said. "My coffeehouse happens to be one of the places where women plot to get into your E.R." His brows rose again, and Shayla nodded. "I personally overheard the scheming, so I can understand why you're overly suspicious. And I really do accept your apology."

"Thank you." His shoulders sank with genuine relief. "Now, will you go out to dinner with me or what?"

Shayla laughed. "You don't give up, do you?"

"Would you believe that Xavier Persistence Wright is on my birth certificate?"

"No."

"You're right. It's Alexander. But it should be Persistence. Keep that in mind, because I'm not giving up on that date."

"Can we get back to the reason I'm here?" Shayla asked.

He put his hand to his chest. "Forgive me. I forgot you didn't come here simply because you couldn't go another moment without seeing me. I need to rein in this wishful thinking."

Shayla laughed. "You are impossible."

"But handsome and charming, right?"

Ignoring his question, she continued. "I'm here, Dr. Wright, because . . . well . . . I was hoping I could enlist your help with a project I've been mulling over for a while. Something you said the other day at the outlet mall sparked an idea."

She'd rehearsed her spiel a couple of times this morning, but now that she was face-to-face with him, she wasn't as sure of herself. The bathroom mirror didn't have quite the same presence.

She grabbed the container of breakfast bars from the shelf and offered him one.

"Breakfast bar?"

He declined with a shake of his head. "The coffee is fine."

Shayla decided to stop stalling. She'd faced a conference room full of the top executives of one of the country's largest coffee chains on a weekly basis. She could ask a simple favor of a small-town E.R. doctor. A very *hot* small-town E.R. doctor.

"Okay," she started. "I know you've only been here a few weeks —"

"Actually, last Friday made a month," he said as he added more coffee to his mug. "One down, two more to go."

"You're counting down the days?"

He shook his head, a sexy grin curling the edge of his mouth. "Not anymore. I'm enjoying my time here more and more every day. I think it may have something to do with this sweet little coffee shop I've stumbled upon. Great food, even better service. And the owner . . . wow."

"Anyone ever told you you're an outrageous flirt, Dr. Wright?"

"Yeah, but I've been told I'm an even better date."

Shayla bit her lip to stop herself from laughing. "I won't be able to get through my well-rehearsed pitch if you keep this up. Don't make all that practice I've been doing in the mirror go to waste."

"You've been practicing your pitch?" He perched a hip against the counter. "Now I really am interested. Lay it on me."

Shayla surreptitiously sucked in a calming breath before she began. "You've been here over a month, so I'm sure that's long enough for you to have noticed that the folks here in Gauthier and the surrounding towns have a lot to learn when it comes to living a healthy lifestyle."

"People do enjoy their food here," he said. "I can't really complain. I haven't had to cook a single meal. Someone is always bringing over food." He pointed to her breakfast bars to make his point.

"The problem is the kinds of food people eat, and the way it's cooked," Shayla said. "I visited Kristi's school the other day, and I was appalled at the snacks their teacher served — greasy potato chips and fattening honeybuns."

"Sounds like your typical snack-time treat."

"Yes, that's the problem. This is the perfect age to start teaching kids about healthy food choices, and instead, they're giving them junk."

"The junk is less expensive."

"That's a weak excuse, and it's used far

too often. When I worked for my former employer, I tried to start an initiative to promote heart-healthy eating — not just a couple of low-fat selections that were still pushing the five-hundred-plus calorie range — but truly healthy options with whole grains, antioxidants and other vitamins and minerals."

"I'm guessing that didn't go over well?"

"It didn't go anywhere."

"I assume that's why The Jazzy Bean has such an impressive variety of wholesome foods. It's pretty admirable what you're doing over there, you know. When you combine it with the Zumba classes, your coffeehouse probably does more to promote a healthy lifestyle than most fitness clubs."

"The response to the Zumba classes has been great, but I'm having a hard time getting people on board with eating better. After seeing the garbage that passes for snacks at Kristi's school, I know I just have to do *something.* My mother died of a heart attack when she was forty-six years old. I don't want my nieces falling into that same trap."

"Exactly how do I factor into this?" he asked.

"Well, I was hoping you could be a spokesperson of sorts. You're everyone's favorite new pastime around here. I think people would listen to you."

"Favorite new pastime?" That grin returned. "If I had not already revealed how much of a shameless flirt I am I would pretend to be offended by that."

Shayla affected her best long-suffering look while trying not to laugh.

"I'm sorry." He put both hands up. "And, just for the record, I am not all that comfortable being everyone's favorite new pastime. Unless, of course, I become *your* favorite new pastime."

Shayla tapped her foot while making a show of inspecting her fingernails, the picture of impatience.

"Okay, okay," Xavier said. "No more interruptions. So, you want me to be an ambassador of some sort?"

"Yes," she said, continuing her practiced spiel. "People listen to you. And not just Gauthier's female population. I heard you finally got Mr. Jessup to start taking his cholesterol medication. Merilee said she's been hounding him for years, yet you see him one time and he's swallowing those pills down with his morning orange juice."

"That's what a few high-definition pictures of clogged arteries will do," Xavier said.

He crossed his arms over his chest and leaned back against the counter. Shayla tried to ignore the way the green scrubs pulled taut across his broad shoulders.

"That's why I need your help," she said. "You're a doctor — you can scare people into paying attention."

"I hate to break it to you, but all the pictures of clogged arteries in the world won't get some people to change their lifestyles. You know how many cardiologists smoke? Some habits are just too hard to break."

"I'm expecting an uphill battle. Eating fattening Southern dishes that taste so good it makes you say 'to hell with my health, I'd rather eat and die happy' is a way of life down here. But I want to show people that they can eat good-tasting food and still take care of themselves."

He stared at her for a moment, his expression unreadable.

"You think I'm wasting my time, don't you?" Shayla asked.

"Not at all. I'm thinking you came to the right man."

This time it was her brow that pinched in confusion.

"I started a wellness program in the community where I had my last assignment,"

Xavier clarified. "It was on a Navajo reservation in Arizona that had a high rate of obesity-related diseases."

"Are you kidding me?" She clasped her hands to her chest. "A community wellness program is perfect! That's exactly the type of thing I had in mind."

"In fact, I got an email from the doctor currently overseeing the program just last night. She sent me some stats. The progress people are making is amazing."

It was impossible to restrain the triumphant smile taking over her face. This was just *too* awesome.

"I cannot believe how perfect this is," Shayla said. "I have ideas in my head, but with you already doing something similar, *and* getting great results, I just know this will be awesome."

"Just one minute," he said. "I haven't said I would help you yet."

His words sent her spiraling down from her quick trip to cloud nine.

"You're saying no?" she asked in total disbelief.

"I'm not saying 'no.' I'm saying 'What do I get in return?' "

"I already accepted your apology," Shayla said.

His lips turned up in a devastating grin.

"The price just went way up."

Shayla sucked in a breath. "If you think I will sle—"

"Not that." He quickly cut her off. "Come on now, Shayla. My mother raised me to be a gentleman. That, if it happens at all, would come much later. Well, maybe not *much* later. I consider that a play-it-by-ear thing. However, we can start with dinner tonight."

Her mouth fell open. "I cannot believe you're resorting to blackmail."

"Believe it."

"But you're a doctor. You took an oath to help people."

He sipped his coffee, set the cup on the counter and then leaned back again, crossing his arms over his chest. "I help people every day. What you're requesting goes above and beyond the call of duty. I don't think dinner is too much to ask."

"Why me?" she asked. "With all the women throwing themselves at you — some quite a bit younger than I am, I might add — why are you so determined to get me to have dinner with you?"

Several long, intense moments stretched between them before he finally answered. "Honestly, I'm not sure. Believe it or not, I've never been this forward with a woman. I know I come off as a flirt, but I'm not. I usually take things slowly."

"So what is it about me that has you acting so out of character?"

"I'm not sure." He captured her hand and lazily grazed his thumb over her skin. "I'm asking for a chance to find out. We can start with dinner and see where it leads. Maybe it won't lead anywhere and we can just be friends who chat over your amazing coffee. But I think there's more," he said. "You feel it, too, don't you?"

Shayla tried to think, tried to speak, but all she could do was stare and nod her head in agreement. She couldn't figure out exactly what it was about him, but she knew there was something there. No man had captured her attention so thoroughly and held on to it with the command he had over this past week and a half.

"I think we owe it to ourselves to explore what's going on here." He lightly squeezed her hand. "What do you say, Shayla?"

"I can't," she said after a moment. Disappointment washed over his face. "I mean I can't tonight," Shayla further explained. "I have to bring my niece to softball practice."

"Well, how long does practice last?"

"I'm not sure. This is the first one. But I know I'll be too tired to go home, shower and get dressed for dinner."

"Okay, so tomorrow night. Or the night after that? Just give me a time and place."

The air vibrated with the desire pulsing between them, its sensual haze thick.

"I don't get it," Shayla said. "I can rattle off the names of a dozen women who would be here in a heartbeat, just panting at the prospect of having dinner with you."

Xavier closed the distance between them. Stopping a scant breath away from her, he dipped his head and said in a low, velvety voice, "The only woman I want is standing right in front of me."

His coffee-tinged breath was warm as it brushed across her face, his words intoxicating, causing a heady rush of excitement to arrow through her bloodstream. Shayla tilted her face up the tiniest bit, bringing her lips just that much closer to his.

The backs of his fingers met her cheek, brushing softly across her skin and triggering a smattering of goose bumps to sprout up and down her arms. Just as he started to lower his head, the door to the break room opened.

"Oh, I'm . . . I'm so sorry."

Shayla whipped around, finding Malinda standing in the doorway, her eyes wide. A knowing smile gradually formed on her lips as she took in the scene before her.

"You two have no idea how sorry I am to have to interrupt what's obviously happening here," Malinda said, "but Mrs. Lambert is back with her grandson, Dr. Wright. She said his fever spiked again overnight. I think it may be something more than just the bug that's been going around."

Xavier blew out a deep breath. "I'll be right there."

"I'll let her know." Malinda backed out of the room, that cagey grin still in place.

"Well, that was embarrassing," Shayla said.

Xavier continued to lightly stroke her cheek with the backs of his strong fingers. "You'd just as well agree to dinner," he said. "I've worked enough small-town assignments over the past year to know what Malinda's smile meant."

"That half the population of Gauthier already knows that we were on the verge of making out in the break room?" Shayla offered.

"Pretty much."

She groaned. "I wouldn't be surprised if the reporter for the Gauthier High School newspaper isn't waiting for a quote when I get back to The Jazzy Bean."

"I'd say you can count on it." Xavier laughed. "That's why I must now insist on dinner. People need to see me wining and dining you. I can't have them thinking we're just hooking up. I have a reputation as an upstanding doctor to maintain."

"They'll know you're an upstanding doctor when you help me implement this new wellness program," Shayla pointed out. "By the way, I would love to get my hands on those stats your colleague sent you last night, and anything else you can provide. I can go over them while I'm at Cassidy's softball practice. Any chance you can drop them off to me at the coffeehouse?"

"How do I know you won't take all my info and run?"

She flashed him a grin. "You don't. You'll just have to trust me."

She extracted herself out of his hold, instantly missing his touch. It was for the best. His touch did strange things to her.

"Thank you again for agreeing to help, Dr. Wright. The residents of Gauthier are extremely grateful." She gave him a little wave before leaving him in the break room.

As he rounded the graveled road alongside the school gymnasium, Xavier caught sight of the baseball diamond surrounded by a glistening chain-link fence. He parked his Jeep underneath a sign boasting the renaming of the school as Nicollet F. Gauthier Elementary School. Another sign hailed the Gauthier Pharmacy and Feed Store as the sponsor of the beautification project that was currently under way. Fresh sod was being laid at the far end of the field, and brightly colored flowers surrounded the base of a statue that Xavier could only guess was of the school's new namesake.

He spotted Shayla and her niece standing on the pitcher's mound. The younger girl, Kristi, was a few yards away, sitting on the grass surrounded by toys. Other than the landscapers, they were the only people there.

Before climbing out of his Jeep, he grabbed the folder he'd brought with him from the passenger seat, and then he made his way to the baseball diamond. Even from a distance he could tell Shayla was doing an awful job of pitching to the older girl.

"You may want to put a little more air underneath that pitch," he said by way of greeting.

They both whipped around to face him. Shayla's face immediately broke out in a grin, which made him feel ridiculously happy. What in the world was it about this woman that had him reacting this way over a simple — granted, downright gorgeous — smile?

"What are you doing here?" she asked.

He shrugged. "Thought I'd check out the talent on the softball field."

"Hi, Dr. Wright," Kristi called, waving like crazy.

Xavier waved back, laughing at the huge grin on her face. Apparently he did inspire crushes in young and old alike.

Shayla gestured to the empty baseball diamond. "As you can see, there's not much going on. Practice doesn't officially start for another half hour, but we decided to get a jump start so we could work on Cassidy's pitching."

"Aunt Shayla doesn't know how to pitch," the older girl said.

Shayla's soft brown cheeks instantly reddened. "We're both learning, right, Cass?"

"But you're supposed to *teach* me how to play. How can you teach me if you don't know how to play, either?"

"That's what your coach will do. I'm going to help as much as I can, though."

"My daddy was supposed to teach me how to play," she said, her voice soft and shallow.

Xavier caught the streak of pain that flashed across Shayla's face.

"Oh, Cass," she said, her shoulders dropping in defeat.

Suddenly, nothing in life mattered more to him than making this better for her.

"I can teach her," Xavier said.

Shayla turned to him. "You don't have to do that."

"Yes, please!" Cassidy said.

Xavier held the folder out to Shayla. "Here's the information I promised you on the program we implemented on the Navajo res. Why don't you look it over while I teach the softball player here the fundamentals of the game?"

"Really, Xavier, you don't have to."

"Aunt Shayla, please," Cassidy begged.

Shayla looked over at her niece. "How do you know he's any better than I am?"

It was hard not to laugh at the incredulous expression on the girl's face.

"Fine." She held both hands up in surrender. "Let's see if Dr. Wright knows what he's talking about."

He traded with her, the softball for the documents, and then pointed to where Kristi played with her dolls. "Just go over there and have yourself a seat, Aunt Shayla. I've got this."

As she walked past him, she whispered, "Thank you."

"You're welcome," he whispered back.

Xavier tossed the ball on the ground and walked over to Cassidy.

"First thing we need to do is get you in the proper stance." He was about to wrap his arms around her, when something occurred to him. "Um, Shayla, you want to come back here for a sec?"

He tried not to stare at her gorgeous legs as she unfolded them from the spot where she'd just sat. It would be easier to run around this baseball diamond a million times without stopping.

She walked up to him, dusting off the backside of her jean shorts. "Giving up already, Dr. Wright?"

"Not at all," he said. "I was going to put her in the proper pitching stance, but I don't want to break any laws about touching a kid that isn't mine."

She grimaced. "I guess that's the world we live in now."

"Unfortunately. I can, however, instruct you on how to do it. Better yet . . ." He paused, mentally high-fiving himself for the brilliance of the thought that suddenly struck him. "I can put *you* in the proper stance."

"Do it, Aunt Shayla. Please," Cassidy said.

"Yes, do it, Aunt Shayla. We need to show

Cassidy how this is done."

She leveled him with a look that said she was onto him, but she didn't say anything as she stepped up to the pitcher's mound.

"First thing's first," he said, stepping up behind her.

God, she smelled good. He pulled in a deep breath, inhaling the light, floral scent of her dark brown hair.

"The one thing you have to remember is that it's all about balance. You need a good, solid center of gravity." Xavier knew he was pushing the envelope, but now that he had Shayla in this position he'd be damned if he wasn't going to take full advantage. He braced his hands on her hips. "Keep it nice and steady."

Shayla tossed a look over her shoulder. "Just what do you think you're doing?"

"Teaching the fundamentals of softball. Keep up, Aunt Shayla." He nodded at Cassidy. "Hand your aunt the ball so we can demonstrate the proper way to pitch."

He wrapped his left arm around her middle and flattened his palm over her stomach. "You want to keep your core nice and tight."

He felt her body shudder and had to suck in a deep breath to stop from doing the same.

"Get your mind out of the gutter, Aunt Shayla," he whispered against her temple.

She peered back at him. "You are so dead."

Xavier grinned. "Can we continue with the demonstration?"

"Yeah, Aunt Shayla," Cassidy said. "I want to know how to pitch before everybody else gets here."

Securing his hold on Shayla's belly, he reached around and captured her right wrist. "Now hold your arm close to your body and swing it back like this," he said, moving her arm back. "It's all in the flick of the wrist when you release the ball. When you come forward, flick your wrist to send the ball spiraling."

As he moved her arm forward, his groin pressed against her backside. He heard an intake of breath and felt another shudder.

"That was a very good release, Aunt Shayla."

"One more time," Cassidy said, picking up the bat.

Shayla pitched again and Cassidy missed by a landslide, swinging the bat a good three seconds after the ball had already sailed past her.

The look on Kristi's face was priceless. She shook her head and went back to her dolls. Cassidy looked as if she was ready to throw in the towel on softball and take up ballet.

"We'll work on it," Xavier said. He gave Cassidy a reassuring pat on the back and guided her to the center of the mound. "Let's see how well you paid attention to your aunt Shayla's demonstration."

He looked back to find Shayla standing with her arms crossed over her chest. She mouthed, *"You're gonna pay for that."*

Xavier mouthed his reply. *"I can't wait."*

Shayla stared at the papers scattered across her kitchen table, paralyzed by the mountain of work that lay before her. This was the stuff she wished she could pass on to Desiree, but even if she did Shayla knew she wouldn't be able to stop herself from going over everything, anyway.

"You wouldn't have to do any of this if you went back to Seattle," she muttered.

How easy would it be to call this whole thing off? To leave The Jazzy Bean in Desiree's and Lucinda's very capable hands? To pack up this house and return to her condo overlooking Elliot Bay? To go back to being the high-powered executive she recognized, instead of this actor trying to fit into a role she wasn't cut out to play?

Sure, it would be easy to pack up and leave. Easy, and cowardly as hell.

Shayla looked over at the refrigerator, where she'd placed the magnet Braylon and Leslie had sent as a Christmas card a couple of years ago. Kristi was still an infant in Leslie's arms, and Cassidy's two front teeth were missing.

A sweet, poignant ache settled in her chest as she focused on Braylon, looking so handsome in his uniform. He'd finished his third tour in Afghanistan just a few weeks before the photo was taken, and had been given special commendation by the army for something he'd done over there.

Her forehead creased as she tried to recall exactly what had warranted the recognition. She remembered it being a huge deal. Braylon had tried to play it off, but Leslie had been so proud, giving Shayla a play-by-play accounting of the ceremony. She hadn't paid enough attention to even remember why her brother had been celebrated.

"Goodness, you suck," Shayla breathed. She ran both hands down her face and pressed her thumbs into her eyes.

Realizing just how much she sucked had been a bitter pill to swallow these past eight months. She'd had her mother for only twenty-one years, but in those years Janice

Kirkland's number one message to her children was the importance of family. She'd taught them to always look out for each other, especially after their father had decided he had better things to do than be there for his wife and children.

How had she allowed her career to overshadow all that her mother had taught her? Of her two parents, how did she end up following her *father's* example?

Shayla pushed up from the chair and walked over to the refrigerator, pulling the magnet down and running a finger along Braylon's face. She followed the path of the birthmark that ran from behind his ear and down his cheek. He'd hated it as a child, until Shayla had told him it was his special mark, the symbol God had chosen to give him to show him that he was unique.

A tear traveled down her cheek, splashing onto the magnet.

What could she have done to save him? How could she have made things better?

Maybe if she had answered his call. Maybe she could have saved her brother's life.

She closed her eyes, picturing the display on her phone with three missed calls, back-to-back-to-back, from Braylon. The image was burned into her brain, her personal torture device.

She could still remember the exact place she was standing when she received the call from Leslie later that afternoon. She'd been in her office, dictating a memo to her assistant while looking out her window at the bumper-to-bumper traffic on I-5 heading south. She had been counting down the minutes until she could leave the office for the weekend in Portland she had planned.

She'd nearly let Leslie's call go to voice mail, but having done so with the previous two, had decided to answer. Shayla wasn't sure if there had been some sixth sense that told her that something was wrong, or if she'd somehow convinced herself of that during the million and one times she'd relived that fateful phone call. One thing she did know was that from the second she heard Leslie's tearful greeting her life would be forever changed.

She caressed her brother's image again. "I'm so sorry I wasn't there to help you. I'm sorry I put everything else ahead of you."

She put the magnet back in its place of honor on her refrigerator door. It was always the first place Kristi went whenever she came over. She loved to say hello to her daddy's picture.

Shayla wiped her cheeks with furious strokes.

Braylon was gone. Tears, no matter how often they were shed, would not bring him back.

Helping Leslie with the girls and developing the kind of relationship she should have had with her brother's family all along — *that* was the best way to honor him. *That's* why she would not take the coward's way out and haul it back to Seattle.

Braylon had done so much in his short time on this earth to make her proud. It was time she did something that would make him proud of his big sister.

Smoothing away the last of the tears, Shayla returned to the table and started stacking the paperwork into manageable piles. Why was she even worrying about this stuff? She was paying an outside accounting firm good money to do this work for her. She didn't have Paxton around to give her a swift kick in the pants and remind her just what she should be doing with her precious time. She would have to do that herself.

Once she'd gathered everything, she loaded it into a cardboard banker box and carried it to her trunk. As she was heading back into the house, she glanced in the car and noticed the folder Xavier had given her this afternoon at the ballpark.

Her mind instantly conjured the sensation of his body snuggled close to hers, his arm wrapped around her waist. Her eyelids fell shut as tiny tremors of need quaked throughout her bloodstream, leaving a tantalizing sensation deep in her belly.

"You really need to stop this," Shayla said as she grabbed the folder and headed back into the house.

But she didn't want to stop. It had been so long since she'd had a man in her life, so long since she'd felt the sensations Xavier had stirred within her.

That was yet another thing she'd sacrificed during her climb to the almost-but-not-quite top of the corporate ladder. She'd allowed her job to consume every aspect of her life, leaving little time for romance. Sure, she'd had a couple of maintenance dates over the years, a few friends-with-benefits relationships with fellow corporate climbers who understood that the road to success did not contain rest stops for relationship nurturing.

But Xavier Wright wasn't the type to call on only when she needed to scratch a certain itch. He was the type of man who drove twenty miles out of his way, just to come over to her coffee shop for a bagel and a little lighthearted flirting. He was the type of man who spent his precious free time volunteering at a health clinic, and teaching her niece the fundamentals of softball. He was the type of man she could see herself falling for.

And that's what scared her the most.

Because he was leaving in just a few short months.

She wasn't concerned about herself — she could deal with a short-term fling. It was all about the girls. They had to be her priority. She was no psychologist, but Shayla knew the absolute last thing Kristi and Cassidy needed was to glom on to a male figure who would eventually leave. Kristi was already smitten with Xavier, and after his help at softball practice, Cassidy, whom she could barely get to say two words to her, could not stop talking about Dr. Wright when she'd brought them to Leslie's.

They were both still coming to terms with losing their father; she couldn't risk the girls being further damaged by losing Xavier after his assignment in Maplesville ended.

Now, for her, on the other hand, Xavier's temporary status was quite possibly the best thing ever.

Knowing he was here temporarily would allow her to manage her expectations. It would eliminate her anxiety over how long things would last, because she already knew exactly how long things would last.

Why not spend the next couple of months enjoying him?

And when he moved on to another hospital in another small town, she'd have memories of their time together to keep her company at night. With all the obligations that took precedence over her love life, she couldn't commit to anything more than what Xavier's temporary status would allow.

He couldn't promise forever, but he could promise right now.

Right now was good enough for her. In fact, right now was perfect.

Shayla snorted. "Yeah, perfectly selfish."

But, goodness, was she supposed to go on like this indefinitely? Wasn't it enough that she'd upended her life? And it wasn't as if her current situation was temporary; she planned to remain in Gauthier through the girls' grade school years, maybe even high school. Was she supposed to go without any pleasure, without any enjoyment for all that time? Punishing herself would not bring Braylon back.

Before she could talk herself out of it, Shayla grabbed her phone from the kitchen counter and texted the number Xavier had programmed into her address book before leaving the softball field.

Would you consider dinner with me at The Jazzy Bean?

Yes! Hell yes! When? Now?

Shayla laughed at his quick reply. It was as if he'd been sitting there waiting for her to contact him.

Not now. Tomorrow?

There was about a thirty-second lull this time. Had to check my schedule. Tomorrow it is. 7 p.m.? Another message immediately followed. Or do you have a Zumba class?

No Zumba. Live jazz on Fridays. See you then.

I can't wait. REALLY can't wait.

She set the phone facedown on the counter and brought her fingers up to her lips, lightly grazing the smile that she couldn't contain even if she tried.

When she'd hastily made the decision to return to Gauthier, romance had been the absolute last thing on her mind. But maybe a little romance was exactly what she needed.

CHAPTER 5

He should be sleeping. He'd been summoned to the E.R. at midnight to fill in for another doctor who'd become ill, and had only left the hospital an hour ago. Yet every time Xavier closed his eyes he was bombarded with thoughts of his upcoming date with Shayla. Of course, those thoughts bombarded him when his eyes were open, too. He couldn't think of anything *but* her.

And he didn't want to.

She'd been a respite these past couple of weeks, the perfect distraction to keep his mind off Nicole. The problem was, Shayla was quickly starting to feel like much more than just a distraction. She was starting to feel like someone who could have him unlocking the dead bolt he'd clamped around his heart.

Was he setting himself up for a hard fall?

Xavier braced his elbows on his thighs and ran both hands down his face.

It wasn't as if this was the first time he'd invited a woman to dinner since his breakup with Nicole. He'd gone out with a fellow doctor, a couple of nurses and that extremely hot pharmaceuticals sales rep in Texas.

But this felt different. This *was* different. He'd gone on those other dates knowing exactly what he wanted to get out of them — a good time, hopefully some good sex and no strings.

Shayla had strings, the thickest of them being those adorable nieces whose company he'd enjoyed way more than he'd thought he would at the baseball diamond yesterday. She was also tied to this area. She'd returned home less than a year ago, but it was more than evident that her heart was heavily invested in the town. Those strings would keep her tethered to Gauthier, while his time here was shrinking by the day.

"It's dinner, not a damn marriage proposal," Xavier said, blowing out an aggravated breath.

Realizing that sleep was not in his future, he changed into running shorts, laced up his cross trainers and went for a jog. Maplesville was small by most standards, though it was obvious the town was in the midst of a massive growth spurt. In the short time he'd been here he'd seen a cupcake bakery and a burrito restaurant open.

As he jogged underneath the canopy of branches arching over the sidewalk, he waved at several neighbors outside doing yard work. He met up with the postman, who'd come into the E.R. last week fearing he was in cardiac arrest, only to leave a few hours later, embarrassed and relieved that it had turned out to be indigestion.

Xavier had seen several patients who'd had the same scare. It probably wouldn't be a bad idea for Maplesville to join Gauthier in the wellness program Shayla had in mind.

Just the mere thought of her triggered a craving deep inside. He didn't want to wait until their date to see her. He needed to see her now.

He reversed course and sprinted back to the apartment.

He changed into brown slacks and a soft blue polo shirt, and a half hour later found himself creeping along Gauthier's Main Street, searching for a place to park.

He'd heard several of the hospital employees talking about the resurgence of downtown Gauthier and how the place came alive on the weekends, but he hadn't expected *this*. The sidewalks were filled with people — more than likely tourists — who

144

moseyed along, dipping into the retail shops.

As he passed The Jazzy Bean, he noticed the outside tables were all occupied. The huge windows revealed a packed coffee-house inside.

He spotted the taillights of a car backing out of a parking spot four storefronts down from The Jazzy Bean and deftly swooped in. Pocketing his keys, he made his way through the throng of visitors, stunned that this was the same sleepy town.

He entered the coffeehouse and immediately spotted Shayla. She hovered at a table that was occupied by a much younger set than the patrons Xavier normally saw here. She looked up and noticed him, and a stunning smile drew across her face.

Yeah, that was his heart skipping a beat just at the sight of her smile. If he thought he could somehow deny that he had it bad for this woman, he couldn't any longer. Not when just her smile triggered that kind of reaction in him.

"Hey there," Shayla said when he approached. She spread her arms out. "Welcome to Jazzy Java Night."

"Impressive," Xavier said. "In fact, I'm impressed with all of Main Street. This place is hopping."

"Amazing, right? It wasn't this way when

I was growing up, but these days little ol' Gauthier is definitely the place to be on a Friday night. And *my* humble establishment has become one of the prime hangout spots."

"That's quite an accomplishment. Congratulations."

She inclined her head. "Thank you very much. I'm rather proud of the way The Jazzy Bean has caught on, seeing as how it went from being a spur-of-the-moment idea to a fully opened coffee shop in less than a month."

His eyes widened. "You don't play around, do you?"

"I spent over a dozen years in the cutthroat world of corporate America. Those who played around got left behind."

His gaze journeyed from her delicately curled hair to the tips of her toes, the nails painted sky-blue, with a daisy on the biggest one. It was hard to correlate the woman standing before him with the idea of the cutthroat corporate executive she described. Yet, looking around the crowded coffeehouse, one couldn't deny the success she'd built, and in such a short amount of time.

She was an enigma. And he was suddenly overwhelmed by the need to figure her out. He needed to know just what it was about her that had him so enthralled.

She pointed at the large clock shaped like an antique sundial. "You're early, aren't you? I thought we agreed on seven?"

He shrugged. "I could say that traffic was lighter than I'd expected, but that would be a lie. Truth is I just really wanted to see you."

The instant blush that stained her light brown cheeks was quite possibly the prettiest damn thing he'd seen in all his life.

"If you were trying to win extra points for saying just the right thing, consider it mission accomplished."

He leaned forward and whispered into her ear, "What do those extra points earn me?"

"I'm not sure I want to reveal that yet. Just keep earning them. It'll be worth it."

Xavier's eyes briefly slid shut against the onslaught of lust her softly whispered words produced.

"Are you hungry?" Shayla asked.

"Starving," he answered, the huskiness in his voice exposing his true meaning behind the word.

Awareness saturated the air between them, so thick he could feel it on his skin.

"Give me a few minutes to check in with Desiree," Shayla said after a few charged moments. "I want to make sure she and Lucinda have everything covered."

Xavier couldn't help but stare as she walked to the counter. She wore a light-colored sundress, along with strappy sandals, like the kind his sister had a million pairs of, and bangles at her wrists. He wondered if she dressed up every Friday night for Jazzy Java Night, or if she'd done so specifically for him.

After a brief conversation with her manager, she returned to him and caught his hand. He registered the softness of her skin, amazed at how much her simple touch affected him.

Their fingers linked together, she led him toward the rear of the coffeehouse. The tables and chairs were arranged in a semicircle, facing an eight-by-four-foot portable stage that had been set up against the back wall. The couch and armchairs that usually occupied that space had been moved to the left.

"Where are we going?" Xavier asked when they bypassed the tables.

"We have an extra special table for tonight's performance."

"Ah, so there are perks to going on a date with the owner."

She looked back at him, a delicious grin curving her lips.

If the God he'd spent his entire life praying to was real, he would end his night with knowledge of how those lips tasted.

Shayla led him to a small alcove just left of the stage. It was hidden from the rest of the coffeehouse's guests by a partial wall. It was set for two, complete with a bottle of wine and candles.

"So, The Jazzy Bean gives up coffee in exchange for wine on Friday nights?"

"We do offer wine and beer on Fridays, but this bottle happens to be from my personal collection. One of my favorite escapes during my years on the West Coast was driving down to Napa."

"Not only do I get to sit at the extra special table, but I get to drink wine from the owner's extra special wine collection? You'd better watch it, Shayla. A man could get used to this kind of treatment."

The earlier blush returned to her cheeks, a deeper shade than before.

Xavier pulled her chair out for her. Moments after they were seated, Desiree came over and placed two small salad plates in front of them.

"Enjoy," she said. "I'll try to get back as soon as I can."

"Don't rush," Shayla said. She turned to him after Desiree had left and said, "I have to apologize for two things tonight. First, there is a very limited dinner menu. If people wanted a gourmet meal they would go across the street to Emile's. The people who come here on Friday nights are here for the jazz."

"I'm here for the company," he said.

"Thank you," she said in a soft voice. "Second, depending on how busy things get, I may have to get up and fix our meal. Desiree, Erin and Lucinda have enough to deal with. I can't have them waiting on me just because I brought a date."

"Shayla, these salads can be the extent of our meal tonight, and this will still go down as the best dinner I've had in over a year. I don't care about the food. You're the reason I'm here," Xavier said, reaching across the table and gliding his thumb over her fingers.

Once again, her cheeks reddened with that ridiculously gorgeous blush. "Another point scored, Dr. Wright."

"I can't wait to cash in these points."

Her lips curved in a sexy smile that was just begging to be kissed. "Neither can I," she said.

Damn. What he wouldn't give to skip dinner and get right to redeeming those points. But the satisfaction of sitting across the table from her was nothing to complain about. As they enjoyed their salads, they talked about her transition from working at a huge coffee conglomerate in Seattle to owning her own small-town coffee shop.

"It sounds as if you were on the fast track. What made you return to Gauthier?"

"Family," she said. "After my brother's death, I felt I needed to be here for Leslie and the girls."

"Malinda told me your brother was a decorated soldier — one of the town's heroes."

She nodded.

"Was it only the two of you, you and your brother?" Xavier asked.

She glanced briefly down at her half-eaten salad before looking back up at him. "My mom died of a heart attack back when Braylon was a senior in high school, and I was a junior in college. Braylon went into the army right after graduation."

"Dad?"

"He may be alive somewhere, but he left when Braylon was still in diapers," she said with a shrug. "My mom has an older sister in north Louisiana, just outside Shreveport, but that's about it as far as family goes. Leslie is an only child, and she doesn't have a huge extended family to help out."

"Was family the only factor that brought

you back?"

"It was the most important, but if I were being honest, I'd have to admit that I was becoming frustrated with the job. It felt as if I'd hit a ceiling with my old company." Another shrug. "When I came home for Braylon's funeral and saw that the old antiques store was available on Main Street, I decided it would be the perfect place for Gauthier's first full-fledged coffeehouse. I called the Realtor and made an offer on the property that very same day. Two weeks later, it was completely cleared out and the kitchen was being put in."

"You really don't play around."

"Actually, I've never done anything quite *that* impulsive, but it felt right." She pointed her wineglass at him. "How about you? How did you become a traveling doctor?"

"What did you say? It was time for a change?"

"That's it? No other reason behind it?"

"Like what?"

"Oh, I don't know. Got tired of working in the big city? Had a falling out with hospital administration?" She set her wineglass down, brought her elbows up on the table and rested her chin on her folded hands. "A broken heart?"

He stared at her for several long moments

before he said, "One of those may have had something to do with it."

Her brow quirked. "The last one?"

He took a sip of his wine. "I plead the fifth."

"Hmm . . . pleading the fifth may cost you a point or two."

"As much as I hate to lose one of my coveted points, I'll have to live with it." He gave his head a small shake. "I just think it's a little too heavy to discuss on a first date."

"Does that mean I'll have to agree to a second date if I want the whole story?"

He grinned. "You see how I orchestrated that?"

"Very smooth, Doctor," she said with a laugh. "Very smooth."

Their food arrived soon after, and the entertainment for the night made his way to the stage. Shayla explained that tonight's saxophonist, Jamal Johnson, also owned the bed-and-breakfast Xavier had passed on his way in from Maplesville.

As they dined on good food and even better wine, Xavier vacillated between bouts of euphoria and outright panic at how much he was enjoying himself. That wasn't supposed to happen. He'd designed it that way.

Everything about Gauthier was beginning

to feel less and less like the benign detachment he'd come to rely on to get him through his temporary assignments, and more like something he could see himself doing permanently, a place he could see becoming his home. The danger in that way of thinking caused his chest to constrict with alarm.

But when he looked over at Shayla, her shoulders moving to the rhythm of the lively jazz, the fear began to subside.

He *wanted* to feel something again. He was tired of just going through the motions, going from one hospital to the next, one town to the next, and never really getting to know anyone. He was tired of being alone. He wanted — he needed — to feel the things Shayla inspired within him.

She caught him staring and smiled, giving her shoulders a playful little shake, encouraging him to join in.

Yeah, he was ready to stop running. And he was starting to suspect he knew the reason why.

They remained at The Jazzy Bean until the second act, a jazz quartet from the local high school, finished their set. When Shayla asked Desiree and Lucinda if they wanted her to stay until closing, they both shot her looks that made even Xavier take a step back.

"Okay, okay." Shayla put her hands up. "I'm going."

"Are you going with her, Dr. Wright?" Lucinda asked.

"I'm going to walk her home," he answered.

"You need to do more than that," she replied.

"Good night, ladies." Shayla tried to talk over her, her cheeks scorching-red. God, she was beautiful when she blushed like that.

They left the coffeehouse and headed north up Main Street. The sidewalk traffic had diminished considerably in the hours since he'd first arrived.

"We could cut through Mr. Douglas's backyard, but he has a couple of schnauzers who use it as their personal restroom. I think it's better we stick to the longer route."

"I have no problem taking the longer route," he said. "It won't be long enough."

Xavier brought their linked hands up to his mouth and kissed the inside of Shayla's wrist, relishing the feel of her delicate skin against his lips.

"Thank you for tonight, Shayla. It really was amazing."

"Dinner and a high school jazz band at my little coffeehouse?"

"It was the best night I've had in a long, long time. I'm not kidding," he said when he caught the skeptical look in her eyes. "Going on a real date hasn't really been on my priority list this past year."

"How long has it been since your last date?" she asked.

"Real date?"

"I guess there's a difference in your book?"

"Yeah, there's a difference," he said. "I haven't been on a real date since I broke up with my fiancée."

Her steps faltered. Whether it was from the pebbled walkway leading up to her front porch, or the word *fiancée,* he didn't know.

"Tonight reminded me how enjoyable life can be when you're with someone who truly catches your attention. I'm looking forward to many more nights like tonight, Shayla."

"Xavier . . ." The apprehension he heard in her voice halted his footsteps.

"Don't, Shayla. Don't push me away."

"It's not that I want to," she said. "But I have to."

Capturing her shoulders, Xavier turned her to face him. "Why? Tonight was amazing. You can't deny that."

"I know it was. I haven't enjoyed myself

this much in . . . I can't even remember how long."

"So, what's the problem?"

"You're leaving," she said. She closed her eyes for a brief moment. "Look, Xavier, tonight was . . . it was even better than I thought it would be. But seeing you on a regular basis, dating you? I just don't know if I can do that. As much as I would love to see where this could lead, I have to think about more than just myself. I need to consider the girls."

"But I think Cassidy and Kristi are great. And in case you didn't recognize it at the ballpark yesterday, they happen to like me, too."

"Yes, they do, and that's part of the problem."

He shook his head. "Shayla, you're not making sense."

She grabbed his hand and pulled him toward the house. The motion-sensor security lights came on as they climbed the steps. Shayla walked them to the swing that hung off to the right side of the porch, but she didn't sit. Instead, she turned to him and said, "You have to understand something, with every decision I make, I have to think in terms of how it will affect the girls.

"It's only been nine months since they lost

their father. I know everyone says that kids are resilient, but I think it's still too soon to bring another man into their lives, especially knowing you're going to leave. If they get too attached to you that can be devastating."

Xavier pitched his head back and shut his eyes tight against her words. She was making too much sense now.

It wasn't out of the realm of possibility that her nieces could look at him in a fatherly way if he started hanging out with Shayla a lot. Especially Kristi. She already clung to him whenever he was around.

It would be wrong — irresponsible even — to allow those girls to get attached to him, take off for his next assignment and leave Shayla to pick up the pieces.

But, dammit, he didn't want this to be their only night together. He couldn't give her up this soon.

Shayla rested her head on his shoulder and released a sigh.

"If I was the only one I had to consider, it wouldn't even be a question," she said. "But my top priority has to be what's best for my nieces."

Xavier drew his hands up her spine and settled his fingers at the base of her head. Lifting her head, he looked her in the eyes.

"You're not with the girls 24/7. I'm willing to take whatever time you can spare for me, Shayla. I don't want to get in the way of the relationship you're trying to build with your nieces, but I also don't want to miss out on what can be the best thing that's happened to me in a long time."

Shayla stared at him, her eyes filled with wonder. She shook her head, and in an awed voice, asked, "How do you do it? How do you always know the right thing to say?"

Xavier tucked his hand underneath her chin and tilted her face up to meet his. "That's because *this* is right."

He lowered his head and slowly trailed his tongue along the seam of her soft lips, coaxing them to part for him. When they did, his tongue stole inside her warm mouth, licking the inside, soaking in her delicate, unique flavor.

A soft murmur floated from her throat, and the sound sent an arrow of desire straight to his groin. Xavier guided her to the shadowy area of the porch and backed her up against the house. He braced his hands on either side of her head and plunged his tongue inside her mouth.

God, but she tasted good. And she felt amazing. Her just-right-for-him breasts pressed against his chest, her nipples rock-hard against him. He hesitated for only the briefest moment before capturing her left breast and rubbing his palm in small circles against her erect nipple.

Her moan encouraged him to go further, kiss her deeper. She locked her arms around his neck and tugged, pulling his head down.

"Come inside with me," she whispered against his lips.

There was a God and He loved Xavier Alexander Wright.

Or maybe not.

The vibrating in his pants pocket was like a cartoon anvil falling from the sky onto his perfect night.

"Son of a bitch," Xavier whispered.

"What's wrong?" Shayla asked.

He reached into his pocket and pulled out the phone.

Dammit. Just as he'd feared.

"I have to go in," he said, unable to mask the irritation in his tone. "There was an MVA involving teenagers on Highway 421, multiple injuries."

"Go," Shayla said, giving him a push.

In this moment he hated his job. "I'm sorry."

"Not as sorry as those kids or their parents," she said. "Do you need me to drive you back to your car?"

"By the time you go inside, get your keys and make the block, I can jog there."

"Okay." She gave him a swift kiss before giving him another light push. "Now go."

Xavier mumbled a string of curses as he jogged down her front steps, hating Hippocrates and his damn oath with every step he took.

Shayla remained in the shadows, standing just outside the edges of the rays cast by the porch light, watching Xavier's tall form as he cut across Gayle's yard and headed back toward Main Street.

"Good Lord." She put her hand over her heart, which still beat like it was in the middle of running the Kentucky Derby.

Shayla staggered over to the porch steps on shaky legs and lowered herself onto the top step. She pulled her cell phone from the wristlet clutch still dangling from her wrist and pulled up Paxton's number. Her friend answered on the very first ring.

"I was just about to call you," Paxton said without preamble. "How'd your date go?"

"Dr. Hottie just kissed the hell out of me on my front porch," Shayla answered.

Paxton's scream was so loud Shayla was sure if she put her phone down she would still hear it all the way from Little Rock.

"I want every freaking detail. And I mean all of it. Size, shape, circumcised or not."

"I said we kissed!" Shayla cut her off. "I don't know anything about size and shape."

Except what she'd felt pressed against her stomach as he'd flattened her up against her house and kissed the ever-living daylights out of her.

"Dammit, Shayla," Paxton screeched. "Don't tell me you had that man's tongue in your mouth and stopped him? You need to give up the martyr role and get some before everything dries up."

"Does your mother know you talk the way you do?"

"Who do you think I get it from?"

Shayla rolled her eyes. "Anyway, I didn't stop him. He got called in to the E.R."

"But you were planning to stop him," Paxton surmised.

"No," Shayla admitted. "I wasn't." She sucked in a deep breath, then slowly let it out. "I invited him inside."

"Thank God," Paxton said. "You're finally coming to your senses. It's about damn time."

Shayla leaned her head to the side and rested it against the newel post. "It still feels as if I'm being, I don't know, selfish."

"By enjoying yourself?"

"Braylon can't enjoy himself."

"Oh, Shayla." Paxton's sigh was long and deep. "You and I both know that if Braylon were here right now he would tackle you to the ground and try to make you eat dirt for saying that."

Her mouth tipped up in a sad smile. "He probably would."

"I know that self-torturing brain of yours refuses to let go of this guilt, but you're going to have to eventually realize that Braylon made the choices he made and there was nothing you could do about it. He was sick, Shayla. And, unfortunately, he didn't get the help he needed in time."

"Because I ignored him."

"*You* were not the help he needed. I know you think you can do it all, but you can't. You would not have been enough for Braylon."

"How do you know that? I could have —"

"You could have done nothing, Shayla. If you don't stop blaming yourself for his death, you can just kiss the thought of ever being happy again goodbye. You need to forgive yourself and move on."

Shayla swiped at the tears that had begun to trail down her face. "I'm trying," she whispered.

"Try harder," Paxton said. "I mean it,

Shayla. Stop looking back at what you didn't do and start looking at all the things you still *can* do. Be the aunt those girls deserve. Take that coffeehouse you've created and build a freaking empire. Go to Dr. Hottie, rip his clothes off and have your way with him. Then call me when you're done and let me know what he's hiding underneath those sexy green scrubs."

A burst of tearful laughter sprung from Shayla's mouth.

"And I want more than just a general description," Paxton continued. "I want length, girth, whether it's curved —"

"Oh, my God. Shut *up,*" Shayla said, laughing so much that she nearly choked. The tears she wiped away now were tears of mirth rather than guilt. "Thank you," she said. "I needed this tonight."

"No, you needed to finish what you started with Dr. Hottie," Paxton said. "But I'm happy I rank a close second."

"You sure you can't come home for Easter?"

"How many Easters did you spend in Seattle?"

Shayla rolled her eyes again. "Point taken."

"Don't think I'm done rubbing that in your face," she said. "However, I do have a few things to get out of storage back in

Gauthier, so I may surprise you all with a quick visit."

Once she ended the call with Paxton, Shayla remained on the porch steps. She brought her feet up a step, wrapped her arms around her legs, and rested her chin on her knees. The brilliant display of stars dotting the ink-black sky was just one of the wonders that made adjusting to life in Gauthier again a bit easier. The stars were never this bright back in Seattle.

It was easy to say she would stop blaming herself for Braylon's death, but she'd been trying to do that for months now. Maybe giving herself permission to enjoy her time with Xavier would be the first step on the road to forgiveness and, eventually, happiness.

She just wasn't sure she deserved it.

Maybe shouldering this guilt was her penance for all those years of being selfish.

"Braylon would want you to be happy," she whispered.

She just needed to figure out what happiness looked like again.

CHAPTER 6

Shayla brought both hands up and massaged her temples. Third-grade math could not have been this hard back when she was in school.

"If you can't figure it out in your head, you can use your fingers," she told Cassidy.

Her niece looked at her with abject horror. "Everybody will laugh."

"I'll bet your classmates are counting on their fingers. They're just sneakier about it."

Cassidy delivered the kind of eye roll only an eight-year-old could pull off. "Maybe I'll just wait until Mommy gets out of the shower."

"No," Shayla quickly said. "I can do this. I mean *we* can do this. Let's put our thinking caps on and figure this out."

Despite the long division–induced headache mushrooming inside her head, Shayla wouldn't give up this quality time with Cassidy for anything. A precious ache squeezed her chest at the thought of how her niece had come to her, that shy, fragile look on her face. When she'd asked for help with homework, Shayla had had to squelch the urge to hug her.

This was what she'd wanted all along. She wanted to be the kind of aunt the girls could call on when they needed help with their homework. She wanted to take them shopping and have slumber parties and bake cookies together. She wanted the kind of relationship that would have her nieces jumping up and down in excitement when Auntie Shayla came over.

She wasn't there yet, but things were slowly starting to come together.

Now, if only she could get her sister-in-law to warm up to her.

Shayla couldn't shake the feeling that Leslie blamed her for Braylon's death. When she'd shared her feelings with Paxton, her friend had told her she was being ridiculous. Maybe she didn't blame her entirely, but there was something in the way Leslie treated her that caused Shayla to believe her sister-in-law held her at least partly responsible.

And why wouldn't she? Leslie had first-hand knowledge of how Shayla had ignored Braylon's many attempts to connect. She couldn't fault her for being wary.

She'd made the bed she was now uncomfortably resting in, but that only made each small victory sweeter. With Leslie's new promotion at work, she'd had to call on Shayla for help more in the past month than she had in the past eight months combined. She would take whatever her sister-in-law was willing to give.

The thought conjured similar words Xavier had spoken to her Friday night, when he'd kissed her stupid on her front porch. He'd told her that he was willing to accept whatever she was willing to give him, too.

Not the time. Her mind should be on long division, not on that man and his incredibly talented mouth.

Cassidy tossed her pencil on the table and pouted. "This is stupid."

"What's stupid?" Leslie asked, picking that moment to return to the kitchen. She had on the ratty blue bathrobe Braylon had worn in high school. It was so old and threadbare; it should have been thrown out years ago. Shayla was happy her sister-in-law had kept it.

"What's going on?" Leslie asked, drying her hair with a towel.

Shayla sighed and ran both hands down her face. "Long division. And, before that, word problems."

"I can't do it and everybody's going to laugh at me." Cassidy got up from the table and ran out of the kitchen.

"Cassidy, come back here," Leslie said. She started after her, but Shayla stopped her with a hand on her shoulder.

"Let me try," she said. "I've been trying so hard to connect with her."

Though she looked reluctant to do so, Leslie nodded.

Shayla went down the hallway to Cassidy's room and found her on the bed with a book in her hand. She knocked on the opened door.

"Can I come in?"

Cassidy's stormy expression would have caused a lesser woman to cower. Shayla took a moment to decide whether or not she was a lesser woman. Deciding it was worth it, she went into the room and sat on the bed.

"Did I push you too hard?" she asked.

After a moment Cassidy shook her head. "I just hate math."

Shayla brought a leg up on the bed and turned to her. "You know who else hated math? Your dad."

Cassidy looked up at her and a small smile drew across her lips. "I know. He always used to tell me to go to Mommy when I needed help with math homework. And one time when I asked him to help me do subtraction with three numbers, he had to use a scratch paper."

"I'll bet. I used to help him with his homework all the time. But you know what?"

"What?"

"He eventually got the hang of it, and when he was in sixth grade, he won a trophy for having the highest grade in his class."

"*My* daddy?"

Cassidy's skeptical look had her laughing.

"*Your* daddy," Shayla said. "Your daddy was very smart. And if he couldn't get the hang of something, he would practice for hours and hours until he got it."

Cassidy's smile dimmed. "I miss him," she said.

"Yeah." Shayla rubbed her back. "So do I."

She looked over at the door and caught sight of Leslie standing in the hallway, her fingers clutching the collar of the threadbare bathrobe, her eyes glistening with unshed tears. Shayla pulled in several deep breaths, willing her own tears to remain at bay.

"So, are you ready to give long division another try?" Shayla asked.

"Can we switch to spelling?"

"You'll have to learn it eventually, Cass."

"I know, but Mommy can teach me."

"Okay." Shayla chuckled. "Why don't you get your spelling tablet?"

Cassidy scooted off the bed. "I want to get my homework finished before Kristi gets home. She always makes too much noise."

"You'd better hurry," Shayla said. "Her teacher said they would be home from the field trip by five o'clock."

Cassidy raced out of the room and to the kitchen. Shayla followed behind her, stopping in the hallway where Leslie still stood.

"You handled that well," her sister-in-law said. "Thanks for telling her that story about Braylon." Her bottom lip gave a slight tremble. She pulled it between her teeth. "We need to talk about him more. I don't want the girls to forget him, but it's just so hard."

"They won't," Shayla said. "We won't let them forget him."

Leslie looked away before looking back at her. "I know I don't say this enough, but thank you, Shayla. I really do appreciate everything you're doing."

Shayla's chest tightened with so much emotion she could hardly breathe. This was the first time Leslie had come close to acknowledging the steps she'd taken to be here for her family. Even though she hadn't done it for praise, Shayla couldn't deny that it felt incredible to hear her sister-in-law express gratitude.

"You're —" she started, but had to stop to take another breath. "You're welcome. I wouldn't want to be anywhere else."

There was a knock on the front door. A second later, Kristi's boisterous voice came barreling down the hallway, followed quickly by her overly energetic body. She threw her arms around Leslie's legs, then turned to Shayla and did the same to her. She didn't give anyone a chance to ask about her trip to the bunny farm with her preschool class, just started an excited dialogue about baby bunnies with furry tails and ears that pointed up whenever they sniffed the air.

Cassidy came into the hallway and rolled her eyes.

It was obvious that spelling words would not be on the agenda tonight, not with Kristi talking a mile a minute and practically jumping off the walls with excitement. Leslie popped popcorn and they all gathered in the family room to watch the Peter Cottontail cartoon DVD that Kristi had won on her field trip.

Shayla hung around the house until the

girls' bedtime, and had to admit that she was as bummed about them having to go to bed as they were. She didn't want to leave. This felt too good, too *right.* For the first time since her move back home to Gauthier, it felt as if she was finally where she belonged.

With her family.

She celebrated another tiny victory when Leslie invited her to help tuck the girls in. They both knew that her help wasn't needed; Leslie's request was yet another sign that things were turning around. The fracture was beginning to heal.

The minute she got behind the wheel of her car, she immediately called Paxton. The phone rang five times before going to voice mail, but Shayla didn't bother leaving a message. A moment later, she got a text from Paxton.

At dinner with new coworker. HOT. May give him my goodies.

Shayla burst out laughing. She texted back: Have fun. I don't want his size details.

I still want Dr. Hottie's!!!

"Yeah, I want Dr. Hottie's, too," Shayla

muttered. Her body was still sending her resentful vibes after her opportunity to learn Dr. Hottie's size had been tragically interrupted. Shayla didn't realize just how badly she wanted it — how badly she needed it — until she'd come so close, only to have it snatched away.

"It would have been so good," she said, tossing the phone on the passenger seat and backing out of the driveway.

She hesitated only a moment before turning in the opposite direction of her house. Twenty minutes later, she pulled into a parking space not too far from Maplesville General's Emergency Room entrance. She shut off the engine but remained in the car, her fingers wrapped around the steering wheel.

She didn't even know if Xavier was working today. And if he was working it wasn't as if he would be able to just leave the hospital simply because she'd decided to show up. And why hadn't she thought about how tired he would be after working all day in the E.R.? And what about —

A knock on her driver's-side window startled her so badly her head nearly hit the car's roof. She looked over and found Xavier standing outside her car, both hands raised in apology.

Shayla sat for another few moments, her palm flattened against her racing heart. He rapped on her window again and Shayla motioned for him to step back so she could open the car door.

"First, I want to make sure you're not here for an emergency," Xavier said as she alighted from the car.

"No," she answered. After a beat she admitted, "I just wanted to see you."

A broad smile drew across his face. "I like the sound of that."

Shayla laughed. She gestured to the backpack he carried. "Are you starting your workday, or ending it?"

"Ending it," he said. He wrapped his arms around her waist and folded his hands at the small of her back. "Do you know how excited I was when I spotted your car on the way to my Jeep?"

"There you go saying all the right things again," she said.

"You make it incredibly easy." He captured her hand and pressed a kiss to the back of her fingers. "Are you hungry?"

"I had dinner with Leslie and the girls."

"And how did that go?"

"It was amazing," Shayla admitted. "So incredibly, unbelievably, fabulously amazing that I'm about to burst out of my skin.

That's why I came here. I was just too excited to go home."

He peered down at her, and with the sexiest grin imaginable, said, "I know one way you can burn off that excess energy."

"You're swinging too soon," Xavier called.

Shayla let the bat drop and plunked her hands on her hips. "You know, when you said you knew how I could burn off excess energy, this wasn't exactly what I was thinking."

"I know, but I thought you needed this more." He stooped down and retrieved the bat. "You want to keep that momentum going with Cassidy, don't you? Think of how cool she'll think you are when she finds out you've been practicing your softball, Aunt Shayla."

"According to my nieces, *cool* is a word old people use," Shayla informed him. "The new word for *cool* is *sick.*"

"Ah, yes. One of the kids I saw at the clinic mentioned that. *Sick* has an entirely different meaning for me. Now stop trying to distract me and let's get back to work."

"It's too hard," Shayla complained.

Xavier trailed his fingers down her arm in a light, teasing caress. "I think you just want me to give you a hands-on demonstration again."

"Hmm, I do find myself thinking about your last demonstration an awful lot. Usually when I'm home alone. Often in the shower."

"Dammit." Xavier hissed through clenched teeth. "Just kill me now, why don't you?"

"Sorry." Shayla laughed.

"Give me that bat," he said. "Now turn around."

She did as instructed, turning her back to him and fitting her backside against his groin. He stifled another groan and tried desperately to control his body's reaction to her. It was, by far, the hardest thing he'd done this week.

"Bend over slightly," he said.

He fitted her against him as he leaned over to grip her wrist. His arousal swelled at the feel of her soft, round backside pressed against him. Shayla gasped, a soft moan escaping her lips.

"The batting cages were a bad idea," Xavier said. "We should have gone back to my place."

Shayla peered at him over her shoulder. "We still can."

That was all the urging he needed.

Xavier snatched the bat from her hand and took her by the wrist. They were in the Jeep and on the highway in minutes, and pulling into the space in front of his garage apartment not long after that.

He motioned for her to go ahead of him up the stairs and had to stop himself from taking a bite out of her firm behind as it bounced mere inches from his face. Shayla moved slightly away from the door, allowing him space to unlock it. The minute he did, they rushed into the small apartment and attacked each other.

Xavier carried her the few steps to the bed and lowered her onto the mattress. She quickly pulled her top off and shucked her jeans down her hips. He followed, stripping out of his scrubs and kicking them away. He thanked God he'd had the foresight to grab a couple of condoms from the bowl Malinda kept in the clinic. It had been too damn long since he'd had to buy them for himself.

He rolled the latex over his erection and lowered himself on top of her, entering with one swift thrust. Diving into her snug warmth was like diving into heaven. His hands braced on either side of her head, Xavier leaned forward and dipped his tongue into her mouth, entering and retreating, matching the rhythm of his hips.

"Oh, my God, this feels good," Shayla said. Her voice, thick with desire, traveled over his skin like a caress.

She wrapped her legs around his hips, crossing her ankles over his backside and urging him to pump faster. Xavier obliged, rocking forward, filling her with deep, powerful thrusts. He reached his hand between them, skimming his fingers along her silky-smooth belly on his way down to the spot between her legs he'd been dying to touch. He brushed his thumb across the thick knot of nerves even as he continued to push inside her.

He trailed his tongue along her jawline, sliding it up to her ear and tugging the delicate lobe between his teeth. He heard her swift intake of breath, which was quickly followed by a moan as he increased the pressure of his thumb, swirling it around her clit.

"Oh, God. Xavier, please."

"Reach for it," he said, adjusting his angle and stroking deep. The sensation of her tight wetness clasping around him, sucking him in, was almost too much to withstand. Xavier clenched his teeth, fighting the orgasm on the brink of exploding through him.

He moved his hand up to her breasts and played with her nipples, rubbing one then switching to the other. He rolled the tight tip between his fingers and lowered his head, pulling it into his mouth.

Shayla gasped. She grabbed hold of the sides of his head and lifted his face up to hers. She plied him with a desperate kiss, plunging her tongue inside his mouth, and sending a shiver of need racing down his back.

Recognizing that he wouldn't last much longer, Xavier hooked his arm underneath her knee and pushed her leg up, driving himself forward in one . . . two . . . three powerful thrusts.

"Oh, God," Shayla cried out. "Oh, God. Oh, God. Oh, *God!*"

"Close," he whispered in her ear. "But I usually answer to *Xavier.*"

Her body shivered as he delivered one final lunge. She clutched his back, her fingers jabbing his skin. Xavier welcomed the pleasurable pain. He wanted to soak in every sensation.

"Oh, my God," she breathed, her head falling back on the pillow. One of her eyelids lifted and she grinned at him. "I should get you for being so cocky, but after what you just did you have every right to be."

He winked. "You're welcome." He planted another kiss on her lips. "I'll be back in a minute," he said, pulling out of her and walking to his bathroom to clean up.

When he returned, he stretched out beside her and kissed her shoulder, loving the feel of her moist skin beneath his lips.

"I hate to disappoint you, but don't expect that every time. It's been a while," Xavier admitted. "I had a lot to make up for."

She twisted around until she faced him, bending her arm at the elbow and resting her head on her hand. "Why has it been a while?"

Xavier motioned to her exposed breasts. "You don't expect me to hold intelligent conversation with those in my face, do you?"

She rolled her eyes and pulled the sheet up to cover herself. He frowned.

"Would you answer the question, please?"

"What was the question again?"

"Why has it been a while since you've done . . . you know . . . *this*?"

He shrugged. "I'm a traveling doctor. It doesn't give me much time to form relationships."

"You still haven't given me the full story on how you became a traveling doctor," she said. "I know it has something to do with a woman."

"I didn't say that."

"You didn't deny it, either." She caressed his jaw. "Come on, Xavier, you can tell me. Who broke your heart?"

He shook his head. "I'm not bringing her into bed with us."

"Well, we can move to the sofa." She started to push herself up, but Xavier caught her by the waist.

"Don't you dare," he said. He trailed his nose up her jawline and peppered her smooth skin with kisses. "You'll eventually get the story, just not tonight, okay?"

Xavier could tell she didn't want to let it go, but blessedly, she nodded. "Okay. Not tonight."

"Now," he said, pushing a lock of her curly hair behind her ear. "There's something I've been meaning to ask *you*. Why didn't you have kids of your own?"

Shayla regarded him with a look of horror. "Where'd that come from?"

"It's something that's crossed my mind. You said you came back to Gauthier to help take care of your nieces. I wondered why you didn't have kids of your own."

"Are you kidding me? Have you *seen* me with my nieces?"

"You're great with them."

"Oh, please." Shayla snorted. "I'm the

most inept caretaker ever. Do you remember how we met?"

"That was an accident, and believe me, I've seen a lot worse than a kid ingesting a little harmless dye."

Her brow tilted up, along with the corner of her mouth. "This from the doctor who wanted to turn me in to child protective services? Whatever could have changed your attitude toward me?"

"Smart-ass," he said, giving her naked butt a squeeze. "I'm being serious, Shayla. You don't give yourself enough credit when it comes to Kristi and Cassidy."

"I think you're giving me way more credit than I deserve." She rested her chin in her upturned palm. "I am happy to report that things are getting better. I'm just sorry I've missed so much of their lives already. It's one of my biggest regrets."

"Just one of them?"

She huffed out a humorless laugh. "I have so many it's hard to keep up with them."

Xavier rubbed his hands up and down her arm. "Does one of them have to do with your brother?" he quietly asked. "I'm not trying to pry. I just get the feeling that maybe there was some unfinished business there?"

Her gaze was trained on him, but Xavier

doubted she was seeing him at all. After several long moments stretched between them, she finally asked, "Do you know how my brother died?"

A cord of unease traveled down Xavier's spine. Cautiously, he answered, "I know he was a soldier. I assumed he died in combat."

She shook her head. "He was stateside. Last summer, after coming home from a family vacation at the beach on the gulf coast, he drove back to Biloxi, parked his car on the same beach where he'd just taken his daughters and shot himself in the head."

Xavier flinched. His eyes fell closed as his heart instantly broke in two for her.

He was amazed that in a town as small as Gauthier, which had a gossip vine as thick as any he'd ever encountered, that no one had bothered to mention exactly how Braylon Kirkland had died.

"He suffered from PTSD," Shayla continued, turning to stare at the headboard.

"How —" he coughed, tried to clear the emotion clogging his throat "— how many times did he go to the Middle East?"

"Three tours in Afghanistan and one in Iraq."

"Damn, Shayla. I'm so sorry."

When she looked back at him her brown eyes were brimming with tears, and Xavier's heart splintered even more.

"He tried reaching out to me," she said. "That very morning he called me three times, but I ignored him." She shook her head. "I'll never know if I could have saved him or not."

"Shayla, don't," he said, his chest tightening with pity at the realization that she'd been carrying this burden for months.

"I was never there for him. Not the way I should have been. I was the older one. I should have stepped up after our mother died."

"But you said Braylon went into the military soon after your mother died."

She nodded. Sniffed.

"So what was there for you to do?" Xavier asked. "Would you have put your career — your entire life — on hold? That's too much to ask of anyone, Shayla."

"Maybe," she said. "But it wasn't too much for me to come home every now and then. Maybe if I had returned home for Christmas or their birthdays, or Cassidy's kindergarten graduation, or even half of the dozen other things Braylon begged me to come home for over the years, maybe things would be different now."

He wished he could do something to ease the pain he heard in her voice, but this was something she would have to work through on her own.

He reached for her, needing to offer her whatever bit of comfort he could. He pulled her against his chest and rested his chin on her head.

"I don't have to tell you that focusing on the past won't bring your brother back. You're here now, Shayla. You're doing what you can for his family. Give yourself permission to let that be enough. If not, you'll never find peace."

"Maybe I don't deserve peace," she said.

Xavier tilted her chin up. "Don't ever believe that. You're a good person, Shayla. None of this is punishment for wrongs you think you've committed." He pressed a gentle kiss upon her lips. "You deserve to be happy."

"Maybe there's some truth to that," she whispered against his lips. "Because at this very moment, I'm happier than I've been in a long time."

CHAPTER 7

"Aunt Shayla, can I have two flavors?"

"That's a lot of ice cream, sweetheart. Are you sure you're going to eat two whole scoops?"

Kristi nodded vigorously, the barrettes at the ends of her ponytails rattling with the movement. With that cute face she could have asked for a dozen scoops and Shayla would have caved.

"Okay, you and Cassidy can both have two scoops. After all, this is supposed to be a celebration, right?"

"I guess," Cassidy said, a slight smile edging up her lips.

A few weeks ago, her oldest niece's response would have been an unintelligible mutter and, if Shayla were lucky, a shy shrug. She'd made great strides in getting Cassidy to warm up to her, due in no small part to all the time she and the girls had been spending together these past few weeks.

Leslie had been placed on a special project at work, and heeding Paxton's advice, Shayla placed the running of The Jazzy Bean into the capable hands of her employees, freeing up her time for what was really important: her nieces. When she wasn't with the girls she was either working on the wellness program or snatching as many stolen moments with Xavier as she could. However, spending quality time with Kristi and Cassidy took precedence over everything, and her efforts seemed to be paying off.

Today's trip to Hannah's Ice Cream, a recent addition to Maplesville's booming retail and restaurant industry, was to celebrate the A Cassidy had scored on this week's math test. Shayla allowed the girls to each choose two flavors of hand-scooped ice cream and treated herself to a waffle cone. After all, she'd suffered through those lessons on long division, too.

Cassidy suggested they sit at one of the covered tables outside the restaurant. Shayla's cell phone rang just as she lowered herself onto the bench. She answered without bothering to look at the screen, figuring it was Leslie calling to tell her that her emergency meeting at work had finally ended.

Instead, she heard a deep, masculine "Hello."

Ribbons of need cascaded over her skin just at the sound of his richly timbred voice.

"Are you on your way from New Orleans?" she asked, settling on the bench. Just before leaving her bed last night, Xavier had told her he was meeting with a fraternity brother who was in town for a dermatology convention.

"I am," he said. "I just passed Hannah's and saw you and the girls outside. Am I allowed to stop over and say hello?"

She looked up and spotted his Jeep on Silver Maple Road.

Shayla hesitated. Over the past three weeks they had seen each other at least once a day — either he would come over to her house if he was volunteering at the clinic or she'd go to his small apartment once she was done at The Jazzy Bean — but never when the girls were around.

The distance she'd insisted be in place between him and her nieces had made for some awkward moments. He maintained that he understood her reluctance to allow Kristi and Cassidy to get too attached to him, but Shayla could tell he wasn't as okay with it as he'd first led her to believe.

The situation had become particularly uncomfortable last weekend, on Easter Sunday morning, when he'd called and jokingly pleaded for an invitation to Sunday dinner so that he wouldn't be alone on the holiday. She'd offered to bring him leftovers, but was unwilling to allow him to join them. She didn't want the girls getting the wrong idea, and wasn't sure how Leslie would feel about another man at the dinner table during their first Easter without Braylon.

The disappointment in Xavier's voice had been obvious, and when she'd come over later that night, he'd been particularly subdued. Regret pooled in her belly just thinking about the hurt she'd seen in his eyes.

With a prayer that she was making the right decision, Shayla finally answered, "Yes, you can come over."

There was a pause before he responded with a simple, but meaningful "Thank you."

Words were unnecessary; they both understood the significance of her concession.

Shayla tracked his Jeep as he made a U-turn and came back toward the ice-cream parlor. He pulled in next to her car in the parking lot and started straight for them.

Her stomach clenched with a fresh burst

of want as she watched his tall, leanly muscled body striding toward her. He was dressed in light brown slacks and a yellow polo shirt that worked perfectly against his warm brown skin tone. He was just as scrumptious in his green medical scrubs. Of course, nothing could top the way he looked when he wore absolutely nothing.

Kristi caught sight of him when he was still halfway to their table. She scooted from the bench and ran over to him. The little flirt's smile was a mile wide. Shayla could only imagine how enamored she would be if Xavier was around on a regular basis; hero worship was written all over her face.

"You all came pretty far for ice cream," Xavier said when he finally made it to the table. "It must be a special occasion."

Shayla was about to speak, but Cassidy beat her to it. "Aunt Shayla's treating us to ice cream because I passed my math test. I got the second-highest grade in the class."

"Second highest in the entire class? That calls for extra sprinkles, don't you think, Aunt Shayla?" he asked.

Shayla looked back and forth between Xavier and Cassidy, stupefied at how instantly open and talkative her niece was when he came around. It had taken her months to get Cassidy to open up to her.

"You mind?" Xavier asked.

"Uh, what?" Shayla asked.

"Extra sprinkles? You mind if I get some for the girls' ice cream?"

"Of course not," Shayla said, earning her excited squeals from Kristi and Cassidy.

Xavier went into the ice-cream parlor and came out a few minutes later with plain vanilla ice cream and a small cup with colorful sprinkles. He divided the sprinkles between Kristi and Cassidy's ice cream cones.

"Aunt Shayla, can we go on the swings?" Cassidy asked, pointing to the playground equipment in the park adjacent to Hannah's.

"As long as you stay where I can see you," Shayla told them.

As the girls set out for the swings, Xavier came around the table and straddled the bench.

"Trying to score some brownie points with the nieces, Aunt Shayla?"

"Sure am," she said. "I'm shameless that way."

"Things seem to be getting better between you and Cassidy. It looks as if your hard work is starting to pay off."

"It is." She nodded, barely able to contain the excitement bubbling inside her. "Did I tell you what happened at Cass's softball game the other day?"

He shook his head.

"I can't believe I forgot to tell you! She scored a run — her first ever! When the game was over, she ran over and gave me the biggest hug. I nearly lost it in front of everybody."

"You should see your face right now. You're glowing. It's beautiful."

Shayla felt her cheeks heat. "I have you to thank," she admitted.

His brow rose, so Shayla explained. "You're the one who told me to stop forcing the issue and let her come to me. That's exactly what I needed to hear. I've tried so many different angles — being the buddy, the cool aunt, the disciplinarian — but I could never get Cass to open up to me. Lately, I've stopped trying to play a certain role. I decided to just be regular old Aunt Shayla. And wouldn't you know *that's* who she's responded to best?"

"That doesn't surprise me at all," Xavier said. He leaned over and kissed her shoulder. "I happen to find regular old Aunt Shayla to be fascinating." Another kiss. "And funny." Another kiss. "And incredibly sexy."

She turned to him and pressed a kiss

193

against his lips. "I think you and Cass have slightly different perspectives, but thank you. I find you fascinating and funny, too."

He let out a sharp laugh. "I know you left off *incredibly sexy* on purpose."

"I figured with that huge ego of yours you would be compelled to show me just how incredibly sexy you are tonight."

"Ah. Well played, Aunt Shayla." He nuzzled her neck. "I think I should add *deceptively cunning* to that list."

"Oh, I'm sure Cassidy calls me that *all* the time." She angled her neck to provide him easier access. "I'll bet she goes around to her friends bragging about her deceptively cunning aunt."

He drew his fingers across her cheek, turning her face toward him and lowering his lips to hers for another kiss, but Kristi interrupted them, her eyes glistening with freshly shed tears.

"What is it, honey?" Shayla asked, scooping her niece into her arms.

"I . . . I dropped . . . dropped my ice cream," Kristi managed to get out between hiccups.

"I told her to be careful," Cassidy said as she ran up to them.

"Oh, that's okay, sweetheart." Shayla pressed a kiss to her forehead.

"I'll get her another ice-cream cone," Xavier said.

Kristi's eyes lit up with naked adoration, and unease prickled Shayla's conscious. The infatuation evident in Kristi's gaze was exactly what Shayla had been trying so hard to avoid. Her thoughts must have shown on her face, because Xavier paused in the middle of rising from the bench.

"That is, if it's okay with you," he said.

Despite the apprehension knotting in her belly, she said, "Of course it's okay. Tell Dr. Wright thank you, Kristi."

"Thank you," Kristi said, her previous frown replaced with a smile that stretched across her face. She scooted off Shayla's lap and grabbed Xavier's hand. Cassidy joined them as they headed for Hannah's.

As she watched them enter the ice-cream parlor, Shayla tried to tell herself that her concern was misplaced. Xavier had less than a month left on his contract at Maplesville General. How attached could the girls really become in less than a month?

If the rate at how quickly *she* had become attached to him was any indication, Shayla didn't want to contemplate what was in store for her nieces when Xavier moved on.

"Have you been taking the potassium pills

every day, Mr. Lewis?" Xavier asked as he examined the results of the blood work he'd ordered on the fifty-two-year-old who was much too young to suffer from so many medical conditions.

"Those pills are so big I can hardly swallow them, Doc. I started eating more bananas."

"That's good, but it's still not enough. You'll have to take the pills along with the bananas," Xavier stressed. "I'm going to have Malinda get you a list of other potassium-rich foods you can eat. It's the only way to get the fluid buildup under control."

Xavier had the distinct impression that his advice was going in one ear and out the other, which meant he'd have to try harder with Frederick Lewis. One thing his grandfather had taught him was to pick his battles, and with a patient this young, Xavier decided it was worth the fight. He'd also been taught that the more trust he could build with his patients, the easier it would be to get through to them.

Of course, his grandfather had been treating some of his patients for nearly fifty years. Xavier was lucky if he saw a patient twice before he was on to the next town.

Remaining detached had been one of the

key reasons he'd taken this position, but lately it had also become one of the hardest aspects of it. He worked so hard to put people on the road to better health, but was never around to see the fruits of their hard labor.

He wrote Mr. Lewis a prescription for another blood pressure medication. "I want you to stop the medications you were taking and give these a try. Often with hypertension you have to go through several types of drugs before you can find the one that works best without having side effects."

As he followed Mr. Lewis out of the exam room, Xavier was once again struck by the fact that by the time Mr. Lewis went through this trial he wouldn't be around to see how the drugs worked for him.

Bruce caught up with him in the remarkably empty lobby. "Now that we have a lull in patients, do you want to grab something to eat at that little coffee shop on Main Street?"

Xavier had to stop himself from shouting yes.

It had been three days since he'd last seen Shayla. One of the other E.R. doctors had come down with a virus that was making the rounds throughout the Maplesville/Gauthier area. As a result, Xavier had been pulling double shifts.

And, because that virus was running rampant, there were a high number of people coming into both the E.R. and the clinic in Gauthier with symptoms. He'd lost count of the number of times he'd been vomited on this week.

As he and Bruce walked down Main Street, Xavier spotted Matthew Gauthier standing underneath the green-and-white-striped awning that covered the entrance to Gauthier Bank and Trust.

"Just the two men I wanted to see," Matt said by way of greeting.

"Uh-oh," Bruce said. "Anytime a lawyer wants to see you, you know you're in trouble."

"It's not the lawyer who wants to see you this time," Matt said.

"Oh, so it's the politician. Even worse," Bruce said.

Matt took it all in stride with an easy smile. "All joking aside, do you guys have a little time to spare? I've got something that I've been working on in the state legislature, and while it's not a done deal, I think it's pretty close. I wanted to run it by the two of you."

Xavier frowned, but he couldn't deny he was curious about what Matt could possibly want his opinion on.

He looked over at Bruce, who shrugged and said, "Fine with me. We were on our way to grab something to eat at The Jazzy Bean."

"Perfect," Matt said. "I managed to leave my lunch on the kitchen counter this morning. I love Tamryn, but my honey struggles in the kitchen."

They walked over to the coffee shop, which was doing a brisk lunchtime service. After several mishaps with her espresso machine, the company had replaced it a couple of days ago. With the amount of people there, it looked as if all of Gauthier was happy to see things back up and running at The Jazzy Bean. Of course, that also meant Shayla was too busy to give him more than a passing smile.

He, Matt and Bruce took a seat at one of the iron tables outside. After a few minutes, Shayla came over.

"Your employees letting you work today?" Matt asked her.

"Did you happen to catch the line at the counter? They have no choice." She laughed. "Can I get you all a drink to start with? Something from the coffee bar now that I have a working espresso machine again?"

"Just iced tea for me," Bruce said. Xavier

and Matt ordered the same, and all three got the special of the day, sliced turkey on a whole-wheat baguette. Xavier allowed Shayla to talk him into veggie chips on the side, but Matt and Bruce both opted for the full-fat ones.

She walked away with their orders, along with his undivided attention. He couldn't tear his eyes from the gentle, yet seductive sway of her hips as she went into the coffee shop.

"Uh, Matt, I guess we can start discussing whatever it is you wanted to discuss as soon as someone returns to planet earth," Bruce said.

"I don't know," Matt said. "Looks as if he's enjoying wherever he is right now."

Xavier could feel the back of his neck heating with embarrassment. "I know I've got it bad," he said. "Sue me. It's been a while, okay?"

Matt put his hands up. "You don't have to explain anything to me. I went right past smitten to full-fledged, down-on-one-knee love fast enough to give me whiplash."

Love?

Xavier wasn't ready to own up to the *L*-word just yet, but he damn sure was in something. *Like?* Definitely. *Lust?* Hell yes.

But love?

No, he couldn't go there. Love came back to bite you in the ass, and that bite hurt for a long time.

"What is it you wanted to go over with us?" he asked Matt, needing a subject change.

"I don't have to tell either of you how much of a godsend this volunteer clinic has been to the people of Gauthier," Matt started. "Not only does it save people time and money, but I do believe it's saving lives. It can be a hardship for some residents — especially our elderly — to get out to Maplesville on a regular basis, so a lot of them just don't do it. They ignore symptoms, or try to self-diagnose their problems."

"Or use my favorite, Dr. Google," Bruce said with a snort.

"Exactly," Matt said. "One of my first goals when the legislative session began was to secure funding for a permanent health clinic in Gauthier. I think I may be close."

Xavier peered in the window, looking for a glimpse of Shayla. Instead, he caught sight of Erin coming with their iced teas.

"I wanted to know if either of you would be interested in running it," Matt continued.

Xavier jerked to attention. "Wait. What?"

"I know you're both E.R. doctors," Matt

said. "And I know that you're here only temporarily, Xavier, but I just wanted to put it out there. You *are* here temporarily, right? That's set in stone?"

"It's . . . uh . . . complicated," Xavier said.

Although, to be honest, it wasn't complicated at all. His contract with Good Doctors, Good Deeds was as loosely binding as any he could sign. The organization was grateful for whatever time they could secure from the physicians who worked with them. Most agreed to one, maybe two short-term assignments. Xavier had given them more than they had expected.

The contract for his next assignment still sat on the kitchen counter in his apartment, unsigned. He'd glanced at it a few times this past week, but for reasons he couldn't quite grasp, kept putting off signing it. Now Xavier wondered if it wasn't divine intervention, because Matt's proposition had beckoned one of his long-held aspirations to the forefront of his mind.

Ever since those days as a young boy visiting his grandparents in rural Georgia, Xavier had longed for a practice like his grandfather's. He wanted to have generations of families telling fond stories of how Dr. Wright had taken care of their parents, and their children, and their grandchildren.

His grandfather was revered in that town. He was the person residents knew they could always count on. What Matt had just proposed would give *him* the chance to make the same kind of impact here in Gauthier.

Not only that, but it would give him the chance to see where things with Shayla could eventually end up. He'd forbidden himself from thinking about the limited time he had left in Gauthier. Thoughts of moving on to a new town, of leaving Shayla, in just a few short weeks, caused a physical ache to pound in his chest.

Had Matt just provided him with a panacea for his pain?

"How sure are you about this, Matt?" Xavier asked him.

Matt picked up his glass of iced tea. "It's not a done deal, but I'm ninety-nine percent sure we're going to get the funding."

"And once you have the funding, how long until the permanent clinic opens?"

"Are you saying yes?" Matt asked.

A pregnant pause filled the air. "I'm saying . . ." What was he saying? That he was willing to set down roots again? That he was ready to expose his heart after the way Nicole had shattered it? That he was open to becoming emotionally attached, to removing the shield he'd placed around his soul?

Could he really bear to be hurt again?

"Xavier?" Bruce called his name. "Are you saying that you'll take over the clinic permanently?"

"I'm saying that it's something to think about," Xavier answered.

Shayla chose that moment to return with their lunches. Just the sight of her made everything in his life seem a thousand times better.

God, did this woman know how close she was to owning his heart?

She couldn't possibly realize it, because he had not fully comprehended it until the possibility of remaining with her here in Gauthier had been dangled in front of him. He could let himself love her, because leaving her was no longer his only option.

CHAPTER 8

Shayla leaned against her pantry door, staring at the way Xavier's leanly muscled back bunched and undulated as he stood before her stove. She couldn't decide if he looked adorable or just plain edible with her pink-and-white-gingham apron tied around his waist.

"It takes a pretty confident man to wear a pink apron," she said.

He glanced over his shoulder, and the sexy smile on his face made her want to turn the stove off and drag him straight to her bedroom.

"It's the lace trimming that makes all the difference," he said.

Laughing, she walked over to him, wrapped her arms around his waist and pressed a kiss to his back.

"That smells amazing," she said, peering over his shoulder. "What do I have to do to get a taste?"

There was amusement in his voice when he said, "Depends on what you're willing to do."

She ran her hands down the front of his thighs and back up, smiling when she felt his slight shudder. "I think we can negotiate a price we'll both be happy with."

He released a low groan. "You do love to torture me, don't you?"

He scooped up a bit of the garlic butter sauce and blew on it before bringing the wooden cooking spoon to her mouth. Shayla opened and let him slide the spoon between her lips.

"Mmm. Perfection."

"I agree," he said, his gaze on her mouth. He dipped his head and laid claim to her lips, swooping his tongue inside and stroking her mouth. He released her lips and looked down at the saucepan. "Damn, that *does* taste good."

Shayla burst out laughing. "Are you sure this is a heart-healthy recipe? It tastes far too good to be low-fat."

"Isn't the point of tomorrow's cooking demonstration to make food that tastes so delicious people won't believe it's good for them?"

"I just want to make sure it really *is* good for them," Shayla said. "I don't want you pulling a fast one on anybody, Dr. Wright."

He caught her by the waist and pulled her to him again, wrapping his arms around her hips and letting his hands rest on her butt.

"I'm not in the business of pulling fast ones," he said. "Especially when it comes to something I know I'm good at."

"Cooking?" she asked, her brow arched with false innocence.

He grinned. "That, too."

Shayla's entire body heated at the seductive promise shining in his warm brown eyes, but she knew what would happen if she acknowledged it. Not that she didn't want that to happen, but it would have to wait. The Wellness Day program was tomorrow; they needed to prepare for the cooking demonstration.

She stepped out of Xavier's hold and walked over to the refrigerator to get the salmon she'd picked up at the grocery store. She pulled out a package wrapped in butcher paper.

"What's this?"

She turned to find him staring at her, a knowing look smoldering in those alluring eyes.

"No, Xavier. We have work to do."

A lazy grin formed on his face. "I know."

"In the kitchen."

The grin broadened. "We can do it here, too."

"You are impossible," she said, her cheeks burning.

"God, I love making you blush."

She gave him a stern look, trying her hardest not to laugh.

"Sorry," he said. "What was the question?"

"I asked what's this? I thought you were making only the scampi?"

He pointed to the package. "That is the main ingredient in the dish that will quite possibly become your favorite meal ever."

"Sorry, darling, but unless this is the yellow-fin tuna sashimi from Sushi Love in Seattle, it won't be my favorite. I have dreams about that place."

"Sushi?" He grabbed the package of wrapped meat from her. "Sushi doesn't stand a chance against my lamb chops."

Shayla held both hands up. "All I'm saying is you'd better bring it."

"Oh, I'm going to bring it, baby." He smacked her on the backside. "Make no mistake about it."

She dodged his kiss, rubbing the tender spot he'd tapped. "So where'd you learn to cook? Your mom?"

"Yeah, right." He laughed, returning to

the stove. "My mother is the main reason I had to learn my way around the kitchen. On the rare occasion that she was home to cook a meal for her children, my sister and I usually tried to come up with creative ways to get rid of it."

"Well, you did say she's one of the best neurosurgeons in all of Atlanta. You can't expect the woman to do it all."

"My mother belongs in the operating room. Her mother — my grandmother Irma — is the one who taught my sister and me how to cook. Yet another reason I loved visiting her and my grandfather in the summer."

"You know your eyes light up when you talk about him."

"I can't help it. That old man . . ." He shook his head. "Don't get me wrong. I learned a lot from my dad, but he was always in a lab with his face stuck to a microscope. My grandfather is the one who taught me what it means when you're called to serve. He taught me the importance of advocating for your patients and doing everything within your power to keep them healthy."

"He sounds amazing. Does he know you have designs on one day taking over his practice?"

"He does. Not that it matters — he's too damn stubborn to retire. He'll turn eighty years old this year, but he's sharp as they come. I'll probably retire before he lets go of that practice."

"It has to be hard being so far away from him."

He paused for a moment. "He understands why I had to leave."

She tilted her head to the side. "Are you ever going to tell me why you had to leave?"

He stared at her for several long, weighty moments before he reached for her, catching her by the waist. "We have much better things to do than talk about that."

"Like what?" she whispered against his lips. Her pleasure neurons fired in response to the sweet, spicy and oh-so-delicious taste of his kiss.

Xavier pulled back just a touch. "One second." He reached over and turned the fire off under the simmering saucepan. "Okay, now we can do this without burning the house down."

Sliding his hands up the side of her neck, he thrust his fingers in her hair and held her head firm. The power in his kiss, in the way his aroused body pressed against her stomach, triggered a burst of heat within her bloodstream that had nothing to do with the stove and everything to do with the man who'd captured her heart like no other.

Shayla let out a soft purr as his hands traveled south. He clutched her behind and pulled her hard against him. Pleasure, hot and strong and mesmerizing, flowed through her. His kiss was everything, yet it wasn't nearly enough.

She wanted more. She needed more. She needed all of him.

"Let's go to the bedroom," she said.

"I'm not sure I can make it to the bedroom." His deep murmur drizzled down her spine like warm honey. "Besides, there's a perfectly good table right here."

"As much as the thought of having you on the kitchen table turns me on, this is where I serve my nieces their afternoon snacks. I don't want to answer questions about why my cheeks are so red every time we're at the table."

"And we both know how easily you blush," he said with a grin.

He tightened his hold on her backside and scooped her up. Shayla wrapped her legs around his waist.

"The bedroom it is," he said. A seductive smile lifted the corners of his lips. "You had your taste. Now it's time for me to have mine."

■ ■ ■ ■

Xavier stared at the ceiling above Shayla's bed, the mellow glow from the moon muted through the bedroom's sheer curtains. His eyes were focused on the slowly twirling ceiling fan, so he didn't realize Shayla was awake until he heard her husky voice whisper, "Are you up?"

She did a full-body stretch, her smooth thighs rubbing against his. And just like that, his body hardened.

"I am now," he said, pressing a kiss to the crown of her head.

"I walked right into that one, didn't I?" She laughed. "A better question would be how long have you been up? Awake," she quickly corrected.

Xavier chuckled. "For a while," he answered. "It seems like such a waste to spend my time with you sleeping. I'd rather spend it looking at you."

Her sleepy smile stole the breath from his lungs. "I'd say we're making the most of the time we have left together. Have you heard from Good Doctors, Good Deeds? Do you know where your next assignment will be?"

"No," he answered after a beat. He almost told her about his conversation with Matt, but something stopped him.

"Do you see yourself returning to Atlanta?"

"I don't know about that," Xavier said.

Shayla shifted around, facing him. She folded her hands on his chest and rested her chin on them. "It's time for you to fess up. Why did you leave Atlanta? Or, should I ask, who made you run?"

He peered down at her and blew out a huge sigh at the determination he saw on her face. She wasn't going to let this go.

"I was engaged to a woman I'd been dating for about five years," he said.

"And?"

"And we're no longer engaged."

She rolled her eyes.

"What? You wanted to know why I left. That's it in a nutshell."

"You didn't pack up and leave simply over a broken engagement. There has to be more to the story."

"Not really. I didn't want to be in the same town with her. She wasn't exactly the person I thought she was."

"Did she cheat on you?" she asked.

"Not that I know of. She didn't think I was good enough for her. She considered me a slacker."

"A slacker?" Shayla shrieked. "You're an

E.R. physician who volunteers on his days off."

"Maybe *slacker* isn't the right term. *Under-achiever* is more accurate." Xavier stared up at the ceiling. "She left me for a cardio-thoracic surgeon. It's one of the most prestigious specialties and, in her eyes, much more impressive than a lowly E.R. doctor. I'm at the bottom of the totem pole."

There was a weighty pause before Shayla asked, "Are you still in love with her?"

"Oh, hell no." Xavier laughed.

"Good, because your ex-fiancé sounds like an idiot."

"Between the two of us, I'm not sure *she's* the idiot. She's married, pregnant and settled into her perfect new life, while I'm a traveling hobo."

"You are not," Shayla said, playfully pinching his arm. She pressed a kiss to the spot she'd just pinched and asked in a soft voice, "Did you want kids?"

He nodded. "I even considered pediatrics for a while, but decided I'd better stick with something more general if I wanted to eventually take over my grandfather's family medicine practice. That's been my ultimate goal for as long as I can remember." He looked at her and grinned. "I never got around to sharing that with Nicole. I can only imagine how much earlier she would have left if she knew being the wife of a little ol' country doctor was in her future."

"I won't lie, I'm having a hard time picturing you as a little ol' country doctor myself."

"That's what I am now," he said with a laugh.

"You may be working here on the bayou, but I see you going back to the big city when you tire of us simple folk."

Xavier nuzzled her neck. "I'm not so sure about that. I've always enjoyed the simple country life. The town where my grandfather practices is even smaller than Gauthier."

He smoothed his hand up and down her spine, drawing comfort from the feel of her warm skin against his. It was frightening to think of how quickly he'd gotten used to the sensation of her body next to his. It didn't matter whose bed they were in; as long as she was there with him, it felt like home.

"I'm sorry your ex hurt you," Shayla said.

"I'm not. I was devastated when it happened, but I'm happy I saw her for who she truly was before it was too late. Better to suffer the pain of a broken engagement than a messy divorce."

"Well, then I guess I'm not completely sorry, either," Shayla said. "If she hadn't hurt you, you'd be in Atlanta having babies with her. I'd rather have you here in Gauthier, and not just for my own selfish reasons.

"You've been good for this town. There are so many people who would not have gotten the care they needed if not for you." She pressed a kiss to his chest. "You're a good man, Xavier Wright."

"Thank you," he said. "What's my reward?"

"You want a reward?"

"You just laid out all the reasons that I deserve one."

A seductive smile edging her lips, she lifted herself up and onto his lap. She reached between them, wrapped her palm around his rapidly thickening erection and guided him inside her hot, moist center.

Xavier fisted his hands in the sheets, then gave up the fight and grabbed hold of her waist, guiding her movements as she impaled herself on his rigid flesh, pumping up and down.

Shayla spread her palms over his chest and rolled her hips back and forth. "Is this reward enough?" she asked between labored breaths.

"Not yet." Xavier gasped as her tight body clenched around his erection. "But we're getting there."

CHAPTER 9

Shayla scooted into the seat behind the reception table that Mya Dubois-Anderson had just vacated.

"I just need to change her diaper," Mya said, adjusting her adorable daughter in her arms.

"Take your time. I've got this," Shayla assured her.

She turned her smile up a notch when Nathan and Penelope Robottom entered the school auditorium, which was brimming with more people than Shayla could have ever anticipated for the Wellness Day event.

"Thanks so much for coming," she said. "Here's a map of the booths, and a few raffle tickets. We have a ton of prizes, including several very nice first-aid kits and a hundred-dollar gift certificate to the Gauthier Pharmacy and Feed Store."

"What about to your coffee shop?" Nathan asked.

"There are a couple of gift cards to The Jazzy Bean, too," she said, laughing at the broad smile that stretched across his face.

Following the Robottoms was a group of senior citizens brought in from the Council on Aging Center, along with the eight-grade health-science class from Gauthier High School. Their teacher informed her that she'd made Wellness Day a part of their Saturday field trip. Shayla was thrilled at the number of families who had come with their small children. She and Xavier had set up several demonstrations for children, including a belly-dancing class that Kristi was eager to help instruct.

"I'm back," Mya called as she came around the table.

"But you're minus a cute baby girl with chubby cheeks."

"She spotted her daddy and that was the end of mommy time."

Shayla laughed as she rose from the table. "She has Corey wrapped around her little finger."

"It used to bug me, but the further along I get with this one, the less energy I have," Mya said, rubbing her adorable baby bump.

Mya Dubois and Corey Anderson had been the couple everyone envied back in high school, but she'd left soon after graduation. Shayla had gotten the scoop about their rekindled romance from Paxton, when Mya had come back to Gauthier after being gone for fifteen years — the town's first prodigal daughter.

"I heard Phylicia is expecting, too," Shayla said.

"Uh-oh. Who told you?"

"Your grandmother and Claudette were talking about it when they came over to The Jazzy Bean a few days ago. Why, is it a secret?"

"Well, I guess it isn't any longer," Mya said. She motioned for Shayla to come in close and whispered, "Phil and Jamal got married in Vegas last weekend."

Shayla clapped her hands together. "That's awesome."

"Phil wants to keep news of both the wedding and baby under wraps until they visit Jamal's family next week, but I had to tell somebody. I'm so excited for her."

"We'll have to do something special during Jazzy Java Night after they make the official announcement."

Once Mya resumed her duties at the sign-in table, Shayla went around to the other booths set up throughout the auditorium. Xavier had persuaded a number of his colleagues from Maplesville General to donate their time. The demonstrations ran the gamut, from properly testing blood sugar for diabetes patients to eye screenings.

Corey Anderson was giving a lecture on how to prevent injury during sports, which was being attended mostly by the same high school athletes he taught at Gauthier High School. In the booth adjacent to his was a lecture on how to prevent heat stroke. There was even a seminar on how to use smartphone apps to track eating habits.

Shayla walked to the far end of the auditorium and felt her pulse accelerate at the sight of Xavier. He stood before an audience of mostly women — surprise, surprise — expounding on the importance of getting regular checkups in order to prevent the diseases that plagued so many in this area. She stood to the rear of the booth and listened to him give a plug for the clinic.

One of the audience members raised her hand. "Is there any chance we can get that clinic to open more than just a few days a week?"

Xavier hesitated for a moment before answering. "Now, I don't want to get anyone's hopes up, but that may be a possibility. Stay tuned. You'll find out more in the weeks to come."

A possibility? Shayla's brow furrowed. What was he talking about?

"Any other questions?" Xavier asked. "Don't be shy. Feel free to ask me anything."

Shayla saw the moment he realized his mistake as anxiety flashed across his face. His invitation opened up a floodgate of inquiries from the audience. Some were health-related, others were personal enough to make his cheeks redden. She had no idea he was so adorable when he was knocked off his game.

Bruce Saunders walked into the booth carrying the torso of a mannequin with the inside of its chest exposed.

"Looks like our time is up," Xavier said, his relief evident in the way his shoulders dropped. "If you suffer from upper respiratory issues you'll want to stick around for Dr. Saunders's presentation. And don't miss the cooking demonstration coming up in just a little while. Shayla and I have been working on ways to lighten up some Southern favorites."

Xavier pointed to the back and several heads turned. She'd been on the receiving end of a fair amount of jealous looks over the past few weeks. Some of the women who had fought for Xavier's attention were miffed that she'd been the one to catch his eye.

She understood their envy. She would be green as an artichoke if she had to watch him date someone else.

As the crowd dispersed, Shayla made her way to the front of the booth.

"That was entertaining," she said.

"Is that what you call it?"

"Well, it was for me. Do you know how red your face gets when you blush?"

He zipped up the duffel bag he'd brought with him and swung the strap over his shoulder. "You're having way too much fun at my expense." He leaned forward and whispered against her lips, "I think you'll have to return the favor tonight."

Her nipples immediately responded to the husky timbre of his voice, tightening into achy peaks. "That, uh, won't be a problem," Shayla said.

The amusement lighting his eyes implied that he knew exactly what his whispered words had done to her.

"Too bad tonight is still hours away," he said.

Shayla took a step back, needing to infuse a bit of cool into their heated conversation. Too much more of this and she would spontaneously combust.

"I would be upset if Wellness Day wasn't going well," she said. She flung her arms out, encompassing the auditorium. "Just look at this place. I never expected to have this kind of turnout."

"Getting them here was the easy part," Xavier said. "Convincing them to take what they learn and incorporate it into their lifestyles will be harder. But I've seen the way you work, so I know you're up to the challenge."

He dipped his head to kiss her, but Shayla placed her hand on his chest, halting him. "Not out here." She glanced over each shoulder. "I can feel the daggers being aimed at me right now."

He frowned. "What are you talking about?"

"Don't pretend you haven't noticed the resentful looks I get." She poked his chest. "You're leaving me in a tough spot, you know. You'll be gone in a few weeks, and I'll be stuck here dealing with these jealous women. They're probably plotting my demise right now."

He studied her face, his gaze trained on her for so long that Shayla had to ask, "What?"

"Nothing." He shook his head. "Come here." Taking her by the hand, he drew her behind one of the curtained booths.

"Is this better?" he asked.

"Much," she said, wrapping her arms around his neck and tugging his head down. He captured her lips in a kiss that had Shayla's knees growing weak and her limbs shaking.

Several hours later, her entire body shook as he drove his thick erection into her slick, eager flesh. He carried her to new heights, expertly rolling his hips as he plunged and retreated, nearly withdrawing, but then burying himself to the hilt. Over and over he brought her to the edge, only to pull back just as she was ready to go over. Until, finally, with one smooth, deep thrust, he lit her on fire, delivering an orgasm that resonated in every part of her body.

With a cry that echoed around his apartment, Shayla collapsed onto the bed, her limbs weak and quivering from the force of her release. She covered her eyes with her forearm and blew out an exhausted breath.

"God, I'm going to miss that," she said.

She felt the chuckle that rumbled through Xavier's chest. He tunneled his hand underneath her and cradled the back of her head in his palm.

Several moments passed before his silken whisper pierced the air. "What if you don't have to?"

Shayla moved her arm and looked up at him. "What do you mean?"

"I mean, how would you feel if this doesn't end in a few weeks? If I stick around Gauthier for a while?"

She pushed herself up on her elbows.

"Does this have to do with what you said earlier at Wellness Day when you were asked about the clinic being open more days a week?"

"There's been some talk. Matthew Gauthier is close to securing funding that would allow the clinic in Gauthier to remain open permanently. He's looking for a full-time physician to run it."

"And he came to you?"

He nodded and Shayla's heart started to pound.

"But you're here only for a few more weeks. Then you move on to your next assignment, right?"

He gestured with his head toward the nightstand. "My next contract has been sitting over there for the past month. I haven't been able to bring myself to sign it." He shook his head. "I don't know what it is, but this time, this place, it just feels different."

The hope tightening her chest made it

hard to breathe. "Xavier, what are you saying?"

His gaze met hers and held it, making words unnecessary.

But she needed the words. She needed him to spell it out for her, to tell her she wasn't making assumptions that would leave her disappointed if they turned out not to be true.

"Are you saying you would consider living here in Gauthier?" Shayla asked. "Making it your home?"

"I would," he said, his voice soft but resolute.

"But you're an E.R. doctor. Why would you consider running a small-town clinic?"

"I already told you that my dream has always been to take over my grandfather's practice, but who knows when that will happen. If I stay here I can have the best of both worlds. I can continue to take on a few hours in the E.R. in Maplesville if and when I'm needed, and I can have a small practice of my own, just like my grandfather's.

"I'm ready to stop running, Shayla." He cupped her cheek, the pad of his thumb grazing her face. "It took me a while to realize that's what I've been doing. Hopping from one hospital to another, not really setting down roots. It's been the perfect way to exist without risking getting hurt. But I'm tired of just existing."

He levered himself up and braced his arms on either side of her head.

"I need to know how I would factor into your life if I stay here. I need to know that you'll allow me into every part of it."

He was talking about the girls. She knew that with a certainty she felt down in her bones. She closed her eyes, struggling to hold off the tide of emotion that was desperately close to overwhelming her.

"Shayla, you know I would never do anything to hurt you or your family. You have to trust me when I say that."

"I know," she whispered. She opened her eyes. "And I do."

Xavier's chest expanded with the deep breath he pulled in.

"Shayla Kirkland, I vowed never to say these words to another woman ever again, but I think I'm falling in love with you."

She could feel his heart throbbing against her own. The sensation captivated her, the rhythm of their hearts beating as one.

"I've never said these words to any man before, but I think I'm falling in love with you, too."

A reverent look stole over his face as he

leaned over and joined his lips with hers. He proceeded to make the most beautiful love to her, leaving Shayla with no further doubt. She was in love with him.

Even better, she was no longer in danger of losing him.

"You have got to be kidding me!"

"I tried making a caramel macchiato and it got jammed."

Shayla quickly made it to the other side of the bar and inspected the espresso machine — the brand-new espresso machine.

"Did you clean out the nozzle?" Shayla asked, even though she knew better. Erin treated this machine as if it were a newborn baby.

"I did everything I usually do," Erin said. "I really think it's this model, Shayla. I looked up reviews of it when the last one broke, and from what I read online, this seems to be a running issue with this particular model."

Online reviews. Why hadn't she thought to look at those?

Because she'd been in such a rush to get this place opened that she hadn't thought to do something as basic as research the equipment she was buying. What was she thinking back then? She normally would never do anything so irresponsible.

Shayla blew out a sigh. "I already had my meltdown of the day. I wasn't prepared for another one."

"Desiree is out getting the rest of the supplies for Senator Gauthier's event, so you don't have to worry about that anymore," Erin pointed out.

Thank goodness Desiree had taken control of the situation when their supplier called to say they wouldn't be able to deliver the products she needed for Matt Gauthier's catering job. Of course, that meant Desiree wasn't here to deal with this newest crisis.

It astonished Shayla how quickly she'd fallen out of sync with running The Jazzy Bean. Not too long ago she would have felt it her duty to be mired down in every single issue concerning her business, but these past weeks she'd spent focusing on her nieces and spending time with Xavier had freed her of those self-imposed chains.

But this *was* her business. It was her livelihood, and she needed to get back into the mind-set of being an owner.

Unfortunately, a big part of being the sole owner meant that she bore all the cost, and another espresso machine repair would set her back. She was just a few thousand away from depleting her savings, which she'd used to finance most of The Jazzy Bean's expenditures. Her rainy-day fund wasn't nearly as deep as this one, and she refused to draw from her IRA.

The front door opened and Kristi came bouncing into the coffee shop, followed by Cassidy and Leslie.

"Well, isn't this the kind of surprise I needed today." Shayla scooped Kristi into her arms and plopped a loud kiss on her cheek. "What are you guys doing here?"

"Mom said if we helped with cleaning out the kitchen pantry we could have a treat."

"And they chose cookies and hot chocolate from Auntie Shayla's coffee shop over ice cream. You should feel very special. Not much tends to top ice cream."

"I most certainly do feel special," Shayla said. "Let's see what Ms. Lucinda has in the back."

They all filed into the kitchen. Lucinda, who was busy preparing Harold Porter's daily chicken salad, promised to make the girls a special treat after she was done.

"You know what?" Shayla said. "In all this time I don't think I've ever given you girls the official behind-the-scenes tour of The Jazzy Bean. What do you say?"

"Just don't break anything," Leslie chimed in.

"Don't worry. The most important thing in the coffee shop just broke again. They can't do much damage."

As the girls were checking out the industrial mixer, Leslie's cell phone rang. She glanced at it and grimaced. "I need to take this," she said, stepping away.

"Aunt Shayla, why do you like making coffee?" Cassidy asked. "Daddy let me taste it once and it was nasty."

Shayla laughed. "Probably because it's not a drink for kids. But, to answer your question, I like making coffee because I got a job working in a coffeehouse when I was in college and enjoyed it so much that I decided to stick with it."

"I want to go to a college that has dolphins," Kristi said.

Cassidy rolled her eyes. "There are no colleges with dolphins."

"No, but she can learn how to take care of dolphins in college," Shayla said. "What about you, Cass? You know what you want to be when you go to college?"

"I want to be a doctor, like Dr. Wright," she said.

"Oh, I want to be a doctor like Dr. Wright, too," Kristi piped in. "And play with dolphins."

For a brief moment, anxiety inhibited

Shayla's ability to breathe. Had being a doctor always been Cassidy's dream, or was this Xavier's influence? And if it was because of Xavier, how would Leslie feel about it? Would she think he was encroaching on Braylon's territory? And if she did think that way, would she blame Shayla for bringing Xavier into their lives?

Leslie returned, frustration etched across her face.

"Is everything okay?" Shayla asked.

"You know that big project we just celebrated finishing? It just imploded," Leslie said. "There goes my next two weeks. I'll likely have to work weekends, as well."

"What about Bayou Campers?" Cassidy asked.

Leslie's face collapsed. "Oh, Cass." She ran her hand down Cassidy's arm. "I'm sorry, honey, but there's no way I can get out of this thing at work."

"But, Mom!"

"Is this something I can help with?" Shayla asked.

Leslie shook her head. "This is a lot more than you want to take on, Shayla."

"Hey, I took on softball. I may not be ready for the big leagues, but things have been going pretty well, right, Cass?"

Her niece's vigorous nod brought a grin

to Shayla's lips.

"Softball is a piece of cake compared to Bayou Campers," Leslie said. "This is a weekend in Fontainebleau State Park, in a tent, no bathrooms."

Shayla's entire being instantly recoiled. There were some things she just didn't do, and sleeping on the ground was one of them. The thought of no bathrooms was too far from her experience to even comprehend it.

She tried not to make eye contact with Cassidy. She knew if she saw the tiniest plea on her niece's face she would cave, and that wouldn't be good for anyone.

"Please, Tee Shayla?"

Tee Shayla? When exactly did Cass become a master manipulator? She had to know that endearment would wrap around Shayla's heart like a warm, comfy blanket.

But camping?

"Uh, Cass, I don't know about this. I've never been camping before. At least I had played softball in the past, and look how awful I am at that."

"But you're getting better at softball. And our scout leader will be there. She just needs another grown-up to help out." She cast a wounded glance at Leslie. "Mom promised she would do it."

234

Cassidy pouted, something Shayla rarely saw her do.

"Cass, I told you from the very beginning that it was a possibility that I wouldn't be able to chaperone. I'm sure Ms. Morrison will be able to get one of the other parents to volunteer for the campout."

"But you cancelled the last time you were supposed to chaperone."

"Because your father . . ." Leslie's face crumbled.

"I'll do it," Shayla said.

Leslie looked up at her, her eyes glistening with tears. She tried to speak but her voice broke.

Shayla put a hand on her shoulder. "I'll do it, Les."

"Really, you don't have to," her sister-in-law managed to choke out.

"But she wants to, Mom. Let Tee Shayla take your place."

Leslie dabbed at the corners of her eyes with her finger. "You did hear what I said this would entail, right? Bugs, cooking over an open fire, maybe a snake or two?"

"Mom, stop trying to scare her."

"I'm not trying to scare her, I'm trying to tell her what she's up against."

"I want to go camping," Kristi yelled.

"You're not old enough," Cassidy said.

"Will you do it, Tee Shayla?"

This was the absolute last thing she would ever volunteer to do under normal circumstances, but these were not normal circumstances. She would bet the last time Leslie was supposed to serve as a parent chaperone was around the time of Braylon's suicide.

Shayla tried to put herself in her niece's shoes. She was at that delicate age where she understood death, but was still self-absorbed enough not to understand why she had to be inconvenienced because of what had happened with her father.

"So, when do we hit the trail?" Shayla asked.

"Next weekend," Cassidy said, her eyes alight with excitement.

Leslie's were full of apprehension. "Shayla, maybe you should think about this."

"What's to think about? I just have to make sure the girls don't get eaten by bears or fall into a patch of poison ivy, right?"

"There are no bears," Cassidy said. She hesitated for a moment. "Maybe mom is right."

"No. No. I can do it," Shayla said.

Oh, great, now she was actually *begging* to spend the weekend sleeping on the ground with bugs climbing all over her.

Shayla suppressed a shudder.

"Really," she said. "I want to. It'll be fun."

By the look Leslie gave her, she knew that hadn't come out as convincingly as she'd hoped.

Cassidy ran up to her and wrapped her arms around her waist. "Thank you, Aunt Shayla."

"I can't wait to go camping with you," she said. And she meant it. She'd deal with the bugs, and poison ivy, and lack of a toilet if it meant sharing quality time with Cassidy. She thought about all the time she'd already missed with her nieces, those years of focusing on nothing but her career. She had so much lost time to make up for.

She gave Cassidy another squeeze. "I really can't wait, sweetheart."

Lucinda came over carrying a tray. "Who wants cookies and milk?"

There wasn't much in life that could compete with cookies and milk. As the girls followed Lucinda to a table in the rear of the coffeehouse, Shayla turned toward her office. It hadn't escaped her that she still had a broken espresso machine to contend with.

Before she could take a step, Leslie stopped her. "Shayla, are you sure about this?"

"I have never been surer of anything in my life," she said.

Her sister-in-law laughed. "I doubt that, but in any case, thank you. I know how much this means to Cass, and that last time —"

Shayla put her hand up, cutting her off. "I understand. You don't have to explain."

Leslie's eyes once again grew moist with unshed tears. Thank goodness she was able to rein it in. Shayla was seconds from losing it herself.

Leslie hesitated for a moment. "I hate to ask for something else, but I need to go into the office this evening. My supervisor has called an emergency meeting to figure out how we're going to tackle this new issue."

It took some effort to fend off the disappointment that barreled toward her. This was Xavier's first night off in four days. She'd been thinking about diving into his bed with him from the moment she'd woken up alone in hers.

"I'll come over to your place so you don't have to cart the girls home late tonight," Shayla said.

A relieved smile drew across Leslie's face. "Hopefully, it won't be too late." She reached out and grasped Shayla's hand. "Thank you."

Shayla gave her fingers a reassuring squeeze. "You're welcome."

She went to pull her hand away, but Leslie held on to it.

"I know I wasn't the most welcoming person when you moved back home," she started. "But I want you to know how much I appreciate all you've done, Shayla. It hasn't been easy since I lost Braylon, but you've made it . . . I don't know . . . It feels wrong to say better. I think *easier* is the right word. I would have been able to make it on my own with the girls — I was prepared to do that. But I'm happy I don't have to."

Shayla was convinced that her chest would burst with the emotion filling each and every corner. Hearing those words made everything she'd sacrificed worth it.

Once Leslie and the girls left, Shayla spent the next half hour in a heated exchange with the espresso machine vendor. They offered to prorate the cost of her machine and apply the funds to another model. She would do thorough research before she chose the next one.

After she'd taken care of the espresso machine, she sent Xavier a text message telling him about tonight's change of plans. Despite the fact that he was on the job, he called her less than a minute after she'd sent the text.

"What happened?" he asked.

She told him about Leslie's emergency meeting, and about the latest crisis with the espresso machine. When she mentioned the camping trip she'd signed up for next weekend, Xavier laughed.

"You don't seem like the outdoorsy type," he said.

"I'm the complete opposite of the outdoorsy type, but it will mean so much to Cass. She couldn't go on her last campout because it was right around the time of Braylon's death. I want to make this really special for her."

"You will. Just having you there will make it special. You're learning how to reach those girls, Auntie Shayla. Just stick with it."

"You're not upset about tonight?"

"If I say I am, do I come across looking like a selfish bastard?"

She laughed. "If that makes you a selfish bastard, then I guess I'm one, too. I'll miss sleeping next to you tonight," she said, unable to keep the disappointment from her voice.

"Are you spending the night at Leslie's?"

"No, but I don't know how late it'll be before I get home."

"I don't care how late it is. If you're sleeping in your own bed tonight, then I'm sleeping in it with you, Shayla. Well, we'll eventually sleep. Maybe."

She grinned as a delicious flutter moved through her belly. "I'll call you when I'm leaving Leslie's," she said.

"I'll meet you at your door."

CHAPTER 10

Xavier heard a car pulling into the driveway just as he secured the final stake that held the pop-up tent he'd bought at the massive outdoors megastore that had just opened in Maplesville. He dusted his hands off and came from around the back of the house before Shayla could come into the backyard and see what he was up to.

He met her as she was walking to the gate that led to the backyard.

"Hey," she said.

"Hey." He stepped between her and the gate.

She gave him a curious stare. "What are you doing here?"

"I've been working on a surprise for you, but you look like you may be too exhausted for it." He pulled her into his arms and kissed the top of her head. "Been a rough day?"

"The roughest." She looked up at him.

"Termites."

"Termites?"

"Yes. Nasty, destructive little termites. Erin spotted a couple in the storage room this morning. I had an exterminator come in to spray and he discovered an infestation. He had to report it to the Board of Health, and I had to shut down The Jazzy Bean. Immediately."

"Oh, damn, Shayla. I'm so sorry."

"This is just so much more than I ever anticipated. Do you know what it's going to cost to get rid of those termites? It's going to wipe out the rest of my savings." She shook her head. "I don't know what I was thinking. Giving up my job, opening my own business? I've read all the statistics. I know how hard it is for a new business to survive."

"Those statistics don't apply to you. Your business is thriving. Hell, it's doing better than a lot of businesses that have been up and running for decades." He took her hands and brought them to his lips, pressing featherlight kisses to her fingers. "This is a setback, but it doesn't reflect at all on how you run your business. You're doing an amazing job."

"Yeah, well, let's see how well I'll do when I'm closed down for a week."

"They will be lined up at the door waiting for you to reopen. People go to The Jazzy Bean for more than just coffee and pastries, Shayla. It's all about the atmosphere you've created. That's what draws them in."

"You always know the right words to say," she said.

He shrugged. "Happens to be a specialty of mine."

"Well, you're very good at it," she said with a laugh. She lifted her face and pressed her lips to his in a light kiss. "So, now that the whiny portion of the evening is over, what's this surprise you have for me?"

"Why don't you go inside and take a shower while I finish getting your surprise ready."

She went into the house, and Xavier returned to the backyard. He'd covered the ground inside the tent with thick bedding and a dozen pillows of different sizes. It wasn't exactly what she'd get when she was roughing it this weekend with Cassidy's Bayou Campers troop, but tonight wasn't about preparing her for her upcoming camping trip. Tonight was about seduction, plain and simple.

Once everything was set outside, he grabbed the cooler where he'd kept Shayla's special dinner surprise from the floor of his

Jeep, then went into the kitchen to finish packing the picnic basket he'd borrowed from Malinda. He was tightening the lid on the thermos of miso soup when Shayla came into the kitchen.

"What's all this?" she asked, motioning to the picnic basket.

"Part of your surprise."

He took a moment to stare at her. Damn, but this woman could take his breath away even when she wasn't trying to.

She'd dressed in a soft, lightweight pink hoodie set. It covered her from head to toe, yet Xavier found her just as sexy as when she lay naked next to him in bed. Well, maybe not as much as *that*, but it was damn close.

It still amazed him how she'd managed to claw her way past the barriers he'd built around his heart after Nicole had left him. Other women had tried, but they hadn't come close to affecting him the way Shayla did.

"Is my surprise a picnic?" she asked. "A little late for that, isn't it?"

"Because it's not your regular picnic," Xavier said. He grabbed the basket and invited her to follow him out the back door.

They walked outside and Shayla gasped. The eight-by-ten-foot tent sat in the middle of her backyard, surrounded by dozens of thick pillar candles that aided the half-moon in illuminating the yard.

"We're going camping?" she asked, excitement tinting her voice.

"I figured you needed a bit of practice before your big camping trip this weekend."

Shayla's hand flew to her chest. "This is the sweetest thing."

She turned, wrapped her arms around his neck, and planted a swift, deep kiss on his lips. "Thank you," she said. "After the day I've had, I can't think of anything better than spending the night underneath the stars with you."

"I can think of a few things we can do to make tonight even better," he murmured against her lips, loving the way the moonlight turned her instant blush a soft pink. "We'll save that for later." He lifted the picnic basket. "First, a little sustenance."

He set the basket down next to the tent and unzipped the opening, then he pushed aside one of the nylon flaps and motioned for Shayla to enter.

She stepped into the tent and another gasp escaped her lips.

White, silk-covered pillows were arranged in a circle around a short, Japanese-style bamboo table he'd borrowed from Bruce.

The table was set with small plates, chopsticks and a vase holding a single Japanese orchid.

She turned to him, her eyes wide. "When did you find the time to do all this? Weren't you in the clinic all day?"

"Malinda and I took turns coming over to set it up. Whenever either of us had a lull in patients we'd sneak away and get a little more done." He gestured to the Japanese paper lantern hanging from the pitched ceiling. "I thought candles would have been more romantic, but Malinda didn't want to burn the tent down."

"Good thinking," Shayla said with a laugh.

Xavier reached outside and picked up the picnic basket.

"This is so perfect," Shayla said. "It's just what I needed today."

"Actually, you haven't seen perfect yet." Xavier opened the basket and pulled out the black-and-green box from Sushi Love in Seattle.

"Oh, my God!" she cried. "No, you did *not*!"

"You're the one who claimed this place has the best sushi on the face of the planet. I had to find out for myself."

"Oh, my goodness, Xavier." She took the sushi from his hands and held it to her chest, caressing the side of the box. "Oh, I've missed you."

"Are we going to eat it, or pet it?" Xavier said.

"Eat it!"

They lowered themselves onto the pillows and unloaded the picnic basket.

"They know you there, you know? The minute I said who I was ordering this for they knew exactly what to include. By the way, Mr. Tanaka says hello."

Shayla laughed. "Did he tell you to include extra ponzu sauce?"

"Yes. And he also said you would prefer this over sake." He pulled out the bottle of plum wine.

Shayla snatched the bottle from his hands and brought it to her chest just as she had with the sushi.

"I don't even know what to say." She looked up at him, her eyes sparkling with gratitude. "This is the sweetest thing anyone has ever done for me."

"It was my pleasure." He leaned forward and pressed a kiss to her lips. "And your reaction made all the hard work worth it. Now, let's see just how good this sushi is."

As they dined on salmon, albacore and yellowtail tuna, Xavier coaxed her into telling him about her day, starting with the truck that was delivering her brand-new espresso machine getting into a fender bender that delayed the delivery by more than two hours.

"We had to go through the morning rush hour with only brewed coffee for our customers. The news about the termites and having to shut down was just the icing on the cake," she said. She held her fingers together. "I was this close to calling my old boss and begging to get my old job back."

Even though he knew she was joking, an odd feeling filled his chest.

"Then Leslie brought the girls over to the coffeehouse after school and I remembered why I've fallen in love with my life in Gauthier." She gestured at their surroundings. "And then I come home to this! How did you know this was exactly what I needed?"

"I just wanted to do something special for you," he said.

A smile drew across her lips. "Mission accomplished."

God, he *had* to taste that smile.

Xavier leaned over and once again captured her lips in a slow, easy kiss. Her warm mouth tasted like the sweet plum wine they'd enjoyed with dinner. But he didn't need the wine; he could get drunk off her flavor alone.

"Damn, you taste good," he said.

"So do you," she whispered against his lips.

She sat back on the pillows and picked up her wine. "You've ruined me for this weekend, you know? Our tent will seem even more dreadful after all of this."

"I can drive over to the state park and set this one up. You and Cassidy will be the envy of the Bayou Campers."

She laughed. "That's okay. We'll rough it like the rest of the girls in the troop. I appreciate the offer, though."

"Want to show me how much you appreciate it?"

Her eyes smoldered as she drank the remaining wine from the glass and set it down. Together they moved the table to the side and met in the center of the tent, kneeling underneath the lantern. Xavier pulled her close, seizing her intoxicating lips, while his hands roamed up and down her body. He liberated her of her fleece top, tossing it to the side.

"Now yours," Shayla breathed against his lips. She caught the hem of his shirt and pulled it over his head. Then she flattened her palm on his chest and pushed him back onto the array of plush pillows.

Xavier looked on in aroused fascination as she shoved her pants and panties down her legs. He quickly shucked his off, grabbed a condom from his wallet and rolled it onto the erection that had sprung up in record time.

Shayla lowered herself onto his lap and reached between them, wrapping her palm around his cock and guiding it into her soaking-wet heat.

"Damn," Xavier gritted out.

He pitched his head back, his eyes clenching tight as he concentrated on the feel of her hot, tight body cloaking him, drawing him deeper with every pump of her hips. He settled his hands at her waist and guided her strokes, lifting himself up as she came down on him, harder and harder, faster and faster.

Shayla moved her hands to his shoulders and quickened her pace, tiny gasps of pleasure escaping her lips with every roll of her hips. Her breasts bounced inches from his face, just begging for his tongue to take a lick. He pulled one nipple into his mouth, and then switched to the other, going back and forth between her breasts as he continued to thrust his hard length inside her.

He felt Shayla's walls clench around him seconds before she threw her head back and screamed his name. Xavier could only get in another two thrusts before he went off, the force of his climax so strong his entire body shook with it.

Shayla stretched on top of him, her soft breasts flattening against his sweat-slicked chest and her firm legs tangling with his. Xavier drew his hands down her body, settling one at the small of her back while the other cupped her backside.

Shayla released a satisfied sigh. She pressed a kiss to his chest before resting her cheek there. "You know, if camping was like this all the time, I would give up my house and just move into this tent."

Xavier chuckled. "I kind of like that idea. This tent is better than the garage apartment I'm living in right now."

Shayla looked up at him. "Are you planning to stay there indefinitely?"

"I haven't thought that far ahead." Uncertainty tightened his chest as he debated his next question, unsure how he would feel if her answer wasn't the one he wanted to hear. "Why?" he finally asked. "Do you know someplace I can move into? Maybe a cute little red cottage in Gauthier?"

She shrugged her naked shoulder and pulled her bottom lip between her teeth. Her sudden shyness was the most adorable thing he'd seen in ages, and it caused his body to stir to life. God, could he ever get enough of this woman?

"Maybe," Shayla said. "I happen to know the owner. I can put in a good word for you."

"You do that. And if it helps in making the decision," Xavier said, flipping them over so that he was on top, "I can give you another taste of what would be in store every single night."

"Son of a —" Shayla hissed. She stretched a hand out and stopped herself from plowing face-first into the dank walking trail just in time. Why didn't she think to get proper hiking shoes before coming out here?

Cassidy tugged on her shirt. "Come on, Aunt Shayla, we're falling behind."

"I know. I'm sorry, honey," Shayla said as she tried to move faster across the slippery foliage and twigs that made up the trail in Fontainebleau State Park. The downpour this morning hadn't done her any favors, either. It made the ground slick and muddy in spots, which did not bode well for walking in sandals.

It would have helped if the troop leader would have slowed down, but Shayla recognized her as one of the women she'd seen giving her the evil eye the other night when she and Xavier had been out to the movies in Maplesville. She figured she could forget about any kind of special treatment.

Cassidy stopped several yards ahead of her and turned. "Aunt Shayla?"

"I'm trying, Cass, but this ground is slippery." Her niece looked pointedly at the flip-flops on Shayla's feet. "I know, I know," Shayla said. "I should have worn my tennis shoes."

Maybe if Xavier hadn't kept her up half the night she would have had a clearer mind as she'd packed for their camping trip. She did have extra socks in her bag, so at least she'd be able to protect her feet from bugs once they set up camp.

Shayla nearly fell to her knees in gratitude when she spotted the clearing about thirty yards ahead of them, but her relief was short-lived. The minute they arrived at the campsite, the entire troop was immediately put to work. She and Cassidy were assigned to the team in charge of gathering firewood.

Shayla just knew the camp leader had done that on purpose. There were at least a dozen other things she could have done around the campground that wouldn't have had her going back into the woods in her inappropriate shoes.

Once the firewood had been gathered, they were all instructed to begin erecting their sleeping tents. Shayla and Cassidy were paired with another girl, Ashley, who Shayla recognized from the softball team. She was, unbelievably, even more timid than Cass.

"So, what do we do now?" Shayla asked once the tents were set up.

"Now we get to go swimming," Ashley said.

"Oh, that sounds like fun."

"I don't want to go," Cassidy said.

Shayla turned to her niece. "Why not? As hot as it is out here, I wouldn't mind spending the entire weekend in the water."

"The girls will make fun of her," Ashley said.

"Shut up," Cassidy shot with more venom than Shayla had ever witnessed from her.

"Cassidy!" She didn't know what to make of her niece's uncharacteristic behavior. "Cass, is everything okay?"

"Yes," she muttered. Shayla would have been more convinced if she'd said the sky was purple and flip-flops were good shoes for hiking.

"It's because of that thing on her back and her arm," Ashley said.

"Shut *up,*" Cassidy screamed at the other girl.

Her face was red with embarrassment, and Shayla's chest constricted with remorse. It had been several decades since she was an eight-year-old, but she recalled all too well how cruel little girls could be.

Suddenly, Ashley's words registered.

That thing on her back and arm.

The birthmark.

Of course. It explained so much. That's why Cassidy never wore anything sleeveless, even on a day like today, when it was creeping toward ninety degrees. That's why she didn't want to go to the new splash park in Maplesville that time Shayla had offered to take her and Kristi. She was embarrassed by the port-wine birthmark stain that covered much of her back and arm. Just as Braylon had been embarrassed by his.

The scoutmaster's voice called for them to gather at the fire pit. Shayla told Ashley to go on ahead, but when Cassidy made to follow her, Shayla held her back.

Dipping to her eye level, she said, "Look, Cass, if you don't want to go swimming, you don't have to."

"Yes, I do," she mumbled.

"No, you don't. I'll talk to Ms. Tammy. I'll even make up a lie about why you can't swim if I have to."

"Really?" Cassidy asked, hope and disbelief in her eyes.

"Absolutely, baby. Don't worry about it." She smoothed a hand down Cass's hair. "Do the girls make fun of you a lot?"

After a moment's hesitation, her niece nodded.

"Have you told anyone about this? Your teacher? Your mom?"

"Mommy said that I'm fine the way I am and that I shouldn't let what other people say get to me."

Yeah, like that was easy for a third-grader.

"She also said that Daddy had a birthmark on his face and he didn't let it bother him, so I shouldn't let it bother me."

"Oh, yes, it did bother him," Shayla said. "Your daddy hated that birthmark, but there wasn't anything he could do about it when he was little, and he just got used to it. But you don't have to."

Shayla captured Cassidy's upper arms and gave them a squeeze.

"Times have changed since your daddy was a little boy, and there are things that can be done to make your birthmark less noticeable, or even remove it all together."

"Really?"

Shayla nodded. "When we get home, you

257

can discuss it with your mom. I'll bet Dr. Wright could even suggest someone who could do it."

"Mom won't help me," Cassidy grumbled. "She's just going to tell me it's my special mark."

"Well, it is your special mark." Shayla ruffled her hair. "But even without the mark you're still special."

Cassidy looked up at her. "Will you help me, Aunt Shayla?"

The hopefulness and adoration shining through her niece's eyes was like a balm that covered every bit of hurt Shayla had experienced over the past few months. She saw everything that she'd been striving for in Cassidy's expression: love, forgiveness and the one that meant the most to her — acceptance.

She had to take a breath before she could speak. "Of course I will, sweetheart. Of course I will."

The tent's flap door flew open and the troop leader stepped inside. "Do you two plan to join us?"

"Yes," Shayla said. "But I don't think Cassidy will be able to swim. She has a cut on her back and her doctor doesn't want any kind of parasites getting in it."

"Whatever," the troop leader said. She

gave Shayla a head-to-toe perusal before backing out of the tent.

Shayla looked over at Cassidy, who looked back at her with a devious smile. Cassidy winked, and Shayla burst out laughing.

The next morning Leslie and Kristi were waiting outside the front door when Shayla pulled her car into Leslie's driveway. Cassidy bounded out of the car and ran up to her mother, wrapping her arms around her legs.

"Mom, we had so much fun. Aunt Shayla almost got bitten by a snake."

Leslie's eyes widened. "Uh-oh. Sounds like you girls had quite the adventure."

"It was definitely an experience," Shayla said. She looked at Cassidy, whose smile was as bright as the glaring morning sun. "But it was worth it."

"I want to go camping," Kristi said with a huff, followed by an adorable pout.

Shayla swooped her niece into her arms. "Why don't we have a camping trip in my backyard one of these days?"

"Today!" Kristi shouted.

"I think your aunt Shayla may need a break from camping," Leslie said. "Why don't you and Cass go inside and have one of the post-campout muffins we made, huh?"

"Mommy let me put in the blueberries," Kristi said, wiggling out of Shayla's arms.

As she and Leslie followed the girls into the house, Leslie looked over at her and said, "Thanks again for doing this. I was at the office until ten last night. I never would have been able to make the campout."

"Yikes. Ten? And I thought I used to put in long hours," Shayla said. Actually, now that she thought about it, 10:00 p.m. was pretty standard for the old Shayla. Thank God she'd left that life behind. "Did you all finally get the project finished?"

"Yes," Leslie said. "My schedule should get back to normal now."

They came into the kitchen to find the girls stuffing their faces. Kristi's chin was caked with muffin crumbs. She reached for another even though she was still chewing the one she'd just stuffed into her mouth.

"I think that's enough for now," Leslie said. "Why don't you go into the bathroom and wash up. Cass, I told Kristi we'd go to Playland in Maplesville when you got home. That's if you're not too tired."

"I'm not," Cassidy said with a vigorous headshake. "Come on, Kristi, let's go get ready." She helped her little sister off the chair and they started toward their rooms. But then she stopped, turned, ran back to

Shayla and wrapped her arms around her waist. "Thanks again for coming camping with me."

Shayla's throat instantly swelled with emotion. She could *so* get used to these hugs. To think that she had a lifetime of them ahead of her? She wasn't sure she deserved to be so lucky.

"You're welcome, sweetheart." She stooped down and took Cassidy's face in her hands. "I had the best time with you."

Not one to be left out, Kristi ran over and joined in the hug, and Shayla was pretty certain she would burst from the giddiness coursing through her at any moment. She looked up at Leslie and shared a smile.

"Okay, girls." Leslie clapped. "Go and get ready."

The girls sprinted for the back bedrooms.

"Well, it seems as if that camping trip really was an experience for you and Cass."

"It was," Shayla said. "I think we bonded a little."

"I'm happy to see that," Leslie said. "I know how hard you've been trying with her."

"Getting her to open up to me has been, by far, my biggest challenge since I came back home. And it's the thing I've wanted most."

"Cass has always been shy, but when she comes out of her shell, she's an amazing kid. I'm happy she's allowing you to see that side of her."

Shayla peered toward the hallway to make sure the girls weren't within earshot. "I wanted to talk to you about that," she said, motioning for Leslie to follow toward the other side of the kitchen. "I think I may have discovered what's at the root of Cassidy's shyness."

Frown lines creased Leslie's forehead.

Shayla quickly relayed the incident with Cassidy and Ashley, and about the girls in school apparently making fun of her because of her birthmark.

"I remember Braylon going through the same thing when he was younger," Shayla said. "His birthmark was on his face, so kids were even crueler."

"Braylon told me about how he was teased. He also said it was how he became tough, because he had to fight back all the kids who bullied him."

"Yes, but Cassidy isn't Braylon. She doesn't have that same brash personality Braylon had as a kid. She's sensitive."

Leslie's eyes narrowed with censure. She folded her arms in front of her, cupping her elbow in one hand. "I don't need you to tell me about my daughter, Shayla. I think I know her better than you do."

Surprise stiffened Shayla's spine. She was caught off guard by the swift change in her sister-in-law's demeanor.

"I don't doubt that," Shayla said. "But I do know a little about this. I saw Braylon go through the same —"

"And I *definitely* don't need you, *you* of all people, telling me about my husband." Leslie put her hands up. "Look, Cassidy knows how to stand up for herself. Braylon taught her how to deal with bullies."

"But she doesn't have to deal with them the way Braylon did. There are treatments, outpatient laser therapy that is virtually painless. When I explained the procedure to Cassidy she was so excited —"

"You did *what*?"

"I told her about the treatment," Shayla said. "If you would just look into it."

Leslie stepped up to her, patches of crimson mottling her face, her eyes brightening with rage.

"How dare you come into my house and try to tell me what's best for my child. I don't need you planting ideas in Cassidy's head."

"I was trying to help," Shayla said, her own voice growing sharp.

"I don't need your help. Do you know who needed your help? Your brother! That's who! But you weren't there to help him, were you? You didn't have time for Braylon."

Leslie swiftly turned away, walking toward the stove. But then she pivoted and marched up to Shayla again. Getting right in her face, her nostrils flaring, Leslie said, "Do you even know how much you hurt him? Do you have any idea how it made him feel when you would send him to voice mail, or just have your assistant deal with him?

"He was your brother, Shayla! Not some stranger off the street!" Leslie jabbed a finger at Shayla's chest, her face soaked with tears as she choked on the words. "He needed you and you ignored him. I couldn't reach him, but maybe you could have. Maybe you could have helped him, but you were too damn busy with your own life to give a damn about your own brother!"

Shayla flinched with every word Leslie hurled her way. They slashed at her like whips, cutting all those familiar wounds wide-open. She brought trembling fingers to her mouth, but a choked sob still escaped.

Leslie took a step back. Tears streaked her face, but her jaw was rigid, her countenance resolute.

"I didn't ask for your advice. I didn't even ask for you to come here," Leslie said. "I can raise my girls just fine on my own."

Without another word, she turned and stormed out of the kitchen. Shayla remained rooted where she stood, her body trembling with the anguish rushing through her. She tried to swallow past the pain collecting in her throat, but it went too deep, cut too wide.

Movement caught her eye. She glanced up to find Cassidy and Kristi hovering at the edge of the hallway, staring at her with frightened, heartbroken looks on their faces. It was more than she could handle.

She burst into sobs, covering her face in her hands.

"I'm sorry," she choked out.

She grabbed her purse from the counter and raced to her car.

She went into autopilot, backing the car out of the driveway and heading straight for Maplesville. She knew Xavier was working, but she needed to see him. She needed to feel his arms wrap around her, even if for only a moment.

She hardly registered the twenty-minute drive to Maplesville General. She parked in the lot across from the emergency entrance and went into the hospital, her need for

Xavier increasing with every step that brought her closer to him.

She walked up to the nurse's station and saw Patricia, the nurse who had helped her with Kristi when she'd brought her into the E.R. two months ago.

"Hi there," the nurse greeted. "How are those adorable nieces?"

"They're . . . uh . . . they're great," Shayla said. She sniffed. "Is . . . umm . . . is Xavier available, or is he with a patient?"

A frown furrowed Patricia's brow. "You don't know?"

"Don't know what?" Shayla asked, fighting off the dread that instantly slithered down her spine.

"He went back to Georgia."

Xavier gave two light raps on the door before walking into the stark, but spacious hospital room.

"Well, well, well," his grandpa Julius said from the slightly reclined hospital bed in the center of the room. "I think that doctor lied to me. I must be dying."

"Good to see you, too, old man," Xavier said. He walked over to the metal chair where his mother sat and kissed her cheek. He gestured to the bed. "How is he?"

"He's going to be fine," his mother answered. "Thanks for coming."

"I don't know why either of you are here," his grandfather said. He pointed to Xavier's mother. "You told me just yesterday that you had two surgeries lined up for today, and you, young man —" he jabbed a gnarled finger toward Xavier "— should have saved your money. Nobody needed you hopping on an airplane to come play babysitter."

"Actually, I drove," Xavier said, carefully repositioning the computerized monitor stand so that he could get closer to the bed.

"That's even worse." His grandfather grunted. "Driving on that road. Probably didn't get a wink of sleep."

"Are you going to stop complaining long enough to let me hug you?"

That garnered him another grunt, but his grandfather also gave him two solid pats in the middle of his back as Xavier hugged him.

"So, what did the doctor say? Are they sure it was just a TIA?" He looked down at his grandfather with an accusing frown. "You haven't been experiencing stroke symptoms and have just been too stubborn to tell anyone, have you?"

"I'm seventy-nine years old — I don't have to tell anybody anything."

"Stubborn isn't the half of it," his mother

said, rising from the chair and coming over to the bed. "Now that Xavier is here, I'm going to head back to Atlanta. Dr. Clark stepped in for me this morning, but if I leave now I should be able to perform the second surgery." She bent over and gave her father a kiss on the cheek. "I want you to take it easy. And think on what we talked about. *Really* think about it, Dad."

Xavier was taken aback by the rare sternness in his mother's voice. She had never been one to exhibit a huge display of emotion. By the look on his grandfather's face, whatever they'd discussed had caused some tension.

His mother gave Xavier another kiss before leaving him and his grandfather alone.

"Okay, what was that about?" Xavier asked.

"She's just trying to boss me around. Just like her mother used to do."

"Don't you talk bad about my grandma Irma," Xavier warned.

"If she were still here she would be trying to boss me around just like her daughter. As if I can't take care of myself."

"What is Mom trying to do?"

"She wants me to give up my practice."

It was what he'd expected to hear, but a

sympathetic ache still struck his chest. Julius Miller was a proud man, and a dedicated physician. Xavier knew how much that practice meant to him.

His mother had tried to get him to quit after his grandmother had passed away a few years ago, but his grandfather wouldn't hear of it. As much as he'd dreamed of one day taking over his grandfather's practice, Xavier knew that seeing those patients every day was the only thing that had gotten his grandfather through those first dark months as a widower.

This time, however, he agreed with his mother. If his grandfather's health was starting to decline, he would be no good to his patients.

Just as Xavier was about to impart his two cents on the subject, his grandfather shocked the hell out of him, saying, "I'd already decided to retire before this happened."

"You what?"

The old man's mouth drew up at the corners, a shrewd gleam in his eyes. "I'm nearly eighty years old. Don't you think it's time I start having some fun?"

Xavier barked out a shocked laugh. "Well, yeah, I guess so. I just didn't . . . I don't know. I didn't think you were ready."

"I've been ready for a while. I just don't want Ms. Bossy Pants thinking I'm retiring because she told me to."

Yep, like his mother said, stubborn wasn't the half of it.

His grandfather reached over and covered his hands. "Thanks for coming back. I know I give you a hard time, but I'm happy to see you, son."

"You think I wouldn't have come running after hearing you'd had a stroke?"

"No, I knew you'd be here. You're as hardheaded as that one who just left."

"I'm going to take that as a compliment," Xavier said. He pulled the chair his mother had vacated closer to the bed and sat down.

"Don't get too comfortable," his grandfather said. "You have patients to tend to, so you can't stay long."

"My patients are covered."

"Well, I have a cute nurse I've been hitting on and if you're here she's not going to pay attention to me."

Xavier laughed so hard he nearly tipped out of his chair. "I'll make sure I don't interrupt your flirting time."

They spent the next hour chatting about Xavier's last couple of assignments. His grandfather was impressed with the two wellness programs he'd helped to implement. Xavier held off mentioning the opportunity to run his own clinic in Gauthier.

Learning of his grandfather's impending retirement had detonated the future plans that had begun to take shape in his head. The thing he'd always wanted, to take over his grandfather's practice, could now happen. He couldn't wrap his head around it.

His sister arrived just as his grandfather was being wheeled away for more tests. Xavier invited her to lunch in the hospital cafeteria. They both grabbed premade sandwiches from a cooler and headed for an empty table toward the rear of the room.

"How are things in the E.R.?" Crystal asked. "You should be almost done with this assignment, right?"

"Next week," Xavier said. He fidgeted with the plastic wrap on his sandwich before tossing it on the tray and bringing his elbows up on the table. He ran both hands down his face and released an exhausted sigh.

"I don't know what I'm going to do," Xavier said.

"Uh, I'm going to need a little bit more to go on," Crystal replied as she bit into her egg salad sandwich.

He told her about the possible permanent position in Gauthier.

"What about Good Doctors, Good Deeds? Can you just get out of your next assignment?"

"I haven't accepted a new assignment. The contract has been sitting in my apartment for weeks. Something just . . . I don't know . . . something told me not to sign it, and that was even before Matt approached me about running the clinic."

"You've worked with Good Doctors, Good Deeds for more than a year. I'm sure they'll understand that you're ready to get back to a more stable lifestyle."

"I'm not worried about that," Xavier said, fiddling with the salt and pepper packets that had been left on the table by its previous occupant.

"Well, I don't see what the problem is, Xavier. Getting the chance to run your own clinic in Gauthier sounds like a good thing. You've told me how much you like it there."

"I do like it there. And I'm needed there. I've lost count of the number of people who've come up to me on the street just to thank me for the little bit of time I spend working in the clinic."

"And let's not forget that other reason you have for remaining in Gauthier. I'm surprised you've gone this long without mentioning Shayla's name. Lately, you can't go

272

two minutes without talking about her."

He glanced at his sister. A wry smile lifted the corner of his mouth.

"I'd be lying if I said she wasn't the main reason I don't want to leave."

"So what's the problem? This seems perfect."

"I thought it was." He pitched the salt packet on the table and leaned back in his chair. "But everything's changed now. How can I think about running a clinic in Gauthier now that Pop is considering retiring?"

"What does Grandpa Julius's retirement have to do with anything?"

"You know I've dreamed of taking over Pop's practice ever since I decided to become a doctor. I spent my summers working alongside him. And what about his patients, huh? There are people who have been going to him their entire lives. What are they supposed to do now?"

His sister set her sandwich on the tray and reached for his hand.

"Xavier, first of all, Grandpa Julius's patients are not your concern."

"But —"

"There's another doctor who just opened a practice there," Crystal said.

Xavier's head reared back. "Really? Who?"

Crystal shrugged. "I think his name is Lucas or something? I can't remember, but he's been putting in a few hours at Grandpa Julius's practice a couple of days a week. Grandpa has been preparing for this for a while, and he's made sure that his patients would be taken care of."

"Why didn't he tell me about this?"

"Because you were doing your own thing." She nodded toward his phone. "Stop worrying about Grandpa Julius and go back to that person who keeps lighting up your phone screen. She's called twice since we sat down for lunch."

Xavier pressed the decline button on his phone. "She probably wants to tell me about how her camping trip went with her niece. I'll call her later."

He leaned forward and folded his arms on the table. "Just a few months ago I was happy being a nomad. Who would have thought I'd be in this position, trying to choose between two permanent jobs?"

"This should be the easiest decision you've ever made," Crystal said.

He huffed out a humorless laugh. "Easy? Yeah, right."

"Xavier, you're too smart to make stupid moves, and coming back here to Georgia just to fulfill some sentimental dream would

274

be a stupid move."

"But this has always been a part of the plan," Xavier reiterated. He looked up at his sister. "What am I going to do, Crystal?"

His phone lit up once again with an incoming call, and Shayla's name flashed across the screen.

Crystal nodded toward the phone. "I think you already have your answer."

CHAPTER 11

Xavier brought the paper cup to his mouth only to find it empty.

"Dammit," he cursed, dropping it back into the cup holder.

He'd just crossed the Mississippi/ Louisiana border. That put him about forty miles to Gauthier. Could he make it there without more coffee?

He didn't need more coffee to keep him awake. Recalling the distress he'd heard in Shayla's voice when he'd finally gotten ahold of her around midnight was enough to keep his eyes wide-open and make him step on the gas pedal a little bit harder.

She'd tried to tell him about an argument she'd had with her sister-in-law, but was crying so much that he could barely understand. That's why, after making sure his grandfather was okay, Xavier had gotten in his car and driven through the night, guzzling down shitty gas station coffee across three states.

A half hour later, he turned into Shayla's driveway and pulled in behind her sedan. He hopped out of his car and bounded up the stairs that led to her kitchen.

"Shayla," he called, knocking on the screen door. Xavier checked his watch. It was just past 7:00 a.m. on a Monday morning. For a minute he wondered if she was already at The Jazzy Bean, but then remembered it was still closed down because of the termite infestation.

"Shayla!" He put his hand up to knock again when the door opened.

"Xavier? What are you doing here?" She opened the door wider to let him inside.

He'd been gone less than forty-eight hours and already he'd started to miss her. What made him think he could ever leave?

He clutched her upper arms and held her steady, his gaze roaming over her. "Your eyes are a little pink and a bit puffy, but other than that you look no worse for wear. It was still worth the drive to get back here, though."

"Xavier, have you been driving all night? Are you crazy?"

"A little hopped up on caffeine, but not crazy." He gestured to the French press on the counter. "I could probably use another cup."

"Of course," she said. She walked over to the cabinet where she kept her coffee mugs. "Why aren't you in Georgia with your grandfather?"

"Because it sounded on the phone like you needed me more," he answered.

She spun away from the cabinet, her eyes wide. She sucked in a deep breath and ran back to him. She gripped his shirt and pulled him close, their mouths colliding in the kind of kiss he would give anything to come home to every single day.

"Thank you, thank you, thank you," she murmured against his lips, her breath sweet and warm.

"Mmm . . . I really needed that after the night I've had."

"Me, too," she said, wrapping her arms around his waist and laying her cheek on his chest.

He took her chin between his fingers and tilted her head up. "Shayla, what's going on? What happened between you and Leslie?"

Instant tears sprang to her eyes.

Xavier enclosed her in his arms, drawing her tightly against him. He kissed her temple and soothingly stroked her back.

"Come on in the living room," he said.

"Your coffee?"

"Forget the coffee."

She sniffed and wiped her nose as he held her closely to his side. Once on the sofa, Xavier tugged her onto his lap, her back against his chest. He pressed a kiss to the area of her shoulder exposed by the wide collar of her V-neck T-shirt and whispered, "Tell me what happened."

She had to take several deep breaths before she finally began. She told him about the camping trip, and how she'd discovered that Cassidy's birthmark — one like Braylon had — was the cause of much of the little girl's shyness.

"When I mentioned to Leslie that she should look into getting laser removal for Cass's birthmark, she just . . . she lost it. Some of the things she told me were just so hurtful. But true."

"What kind of things?"

She twisted around in his lap and looked up at him. "I suspected that Leslie blamed me for Braylon's death — at least partially. Paxton told me I was being ridiculous, but a small part of me always knew it."

Xavier's jaw clenched. "She blamed you for your brother's suicide?"

"She didn't come out and say it, but she

did say that I wasn't there for him, and that I could have possibly saved him, but didn't."

He had to wait several moments before he could trust himself to speak. "She shouldn't have said that," Xavier whispered against her hair. "It wasn't your fault, Shayla."

He felt the pronounced sigh that shuddered through her. After several long, intense moments, Shayla said, "I know."

She spoke so softly, Xavier wasn't sure he'd heard correctly, but then she continued.

"Braylon called me three times on the morning he committed suicide. All this time I've been telling myself that if I'd just answered one of those calls, maybe it would have changed things. Maybe I could have helped."

She looked up at him. "Yesterday, for the first time since he died, I realized that there was nothing I could have done. It didn't occur to me until I tried to explain to Leslie that Cassidy doesn't have the same kind of personality Braylon had. She's so tenderhearted. It's just not in her nature.

"Braylon used to get teased over his birthmark, too, until he decided that no one would tease him anymore. That's all it took. He went to school one day and told the kids who were bullying him that he was done taking their crap.

"He was so brave, even as a kid. He was also ridiculously stubborn. No one could make Braylon do something he didn't want to do, and no one could stop him from doing something he had his mind set on."

She took a breath. "That morning when he called, he had his mind set on ending it all. I guess he'd just seen too much."

"He was sick, Shayla. PTSD is real. It's not just some idea that's floating out there."

"I know," she said, her voice choking on the words. "He was sick and didn't get the help he needed. That's all there is to it. But I'll always wonder, you know. I'll always wonder what it was he wanted to say to me on the phone." She rested her head on his chest again. "Maybe he just wanted to tell me goodbye."

They sat there holding each other for untold minutes, with nothing but the sound of their breathing and the hum of the window air-conditioning unit to fill the quiet.

After some time had passed, Shayla braced her hands on either side of his hips and pushed herself up. "I need to finish packing."

Xavier caught her wrist. "Packing?"

Her eyes slid shut. "Goodness, after the

incident with Leslie yesterday, it completely slipped my mind that I never got the chance to tell you this. There was no cell phone reception in the woods, so I didn't get a chance to check my email until late last night. There was an email waiting for me from an outfit in Seattle. It's a newer coffee company — a start-up, but one that's doing really well, and they're looking to expand."

An unsettling current traveled through Xavier's stomach.

"What does that have to do with you?" he asked, rising from the sofa.

"Well, before I became an owner of a small-town coffeehouse, I was a big-time coffee executive with a big-time reputation to match. They want to talk to me."

"And you want to talk to them?"

Her silence said it all.

Xavier just stood there, his body suddenly numb. He stared at her, wondering if this was the same woman he'd been with over the past few months.

"How could you even entertain going back to Seattle? What about the coffeehouse you have here, or the wellness program you just started? You can't just leave that behind, Shayla."

Her head jerked back and she looked at

him as if *he* was the one being unreasonable.

"And just what would I be leaving behind if I went back to Seattle? A coffee shop that has sucked my savings dry, and is currently closed down because of termites? A sister-in-law who hates me?"

"Two nieces who love you." He slapped his palm to his chest. "A man who loves you." He started to pace. "*I'm* not even the issue here. I would love you no matter where you lived, but you can't run away from those girls. You've worked too damn hard to earn your way back into your family, Shayla. Don't give up on them now."

"I'm not giving up on them," she said. She grabbed his wrist, stopping his march. "Look at me, Xavier." He brought his eyes to hers. "The likelihood that I'll even take the job is slim. It's something that came up all of a sudden. I just want to see what it's about."

"You know what's funny? Not too long ago, you didn't want me hanging around Kristi and Cassidy because you were afraid of what would happen if they got too attached to me. How do you think they'd feel if their aunt Shayla left?"

Xavier could tell he'd hit a nerve, so he powered on.

"You belong here, Shayla. Those girls need you. There is nothing for you in Seattle. I promise, if you leave and break those girls' hearts, you will regret it for the rest of your life. The regret you feel over Braylon's death won't be able to compare."

"You're not playing fair," she said.

"There is no playing fair when I'm trying to save you from making the biggest mistake of your life."

Her eyes fell shut as she blew out a weary breath. "You're blowing this out of proportion, Xavier." She opened her eyes and looked at him. "I know what I'm doing, okay? You don't have to worry about me."

She stood on her tiptoes and placed a kiss on his lips, then left him standing in the middle of the living room.

He started to follow her, then stopped. What more could he tell her to try to change her mind?

An even better question was, why was he so against this?

He knew why. It was because he was afraid she would go back to Seattle and see all the things she was missing, all the things she'd given up when she'd moved to Gauthier. He'd lived through one woman deciding that he wasn't enough for her. He didn't want to live through yet another one coming to that conclusion, especially one that had come to mean everything to him.

Shayla stood over the opened suitcase, debating whether or not she should drive over to the outlet mall in Maplesville and buy a new power suit. She'd donated all of her business attire to a battered women's shelter before she'd left Seattle. All she owned that was even remotely suitable was the gray-and-black pinstripe she'd worn to Braylon's funeral. She wasn't sure she wanted to carry those memories into a job interview.

She wasn't sure if she wanted the job interview at all.

"You don't have to say yes," Shayla told herself.

She was just exploring all of her options, making sure she didn't close the door on a golden opportunity. With the way things were going lately, she wasn't sure how long she would be able to last in Gauthier. For that matter, she wasn't sure how much she was even wanted here.

This job could be her ticket back to her comfort zone, back to the place where she thrived.

She wasn't giving up! She was keeping her options open.

Shayla tried to ignore the sickening feeling invading her belly as she folded several more pieces of underwear from the laundry basket on her bed and stuffed them into the suitcase. She picked up the threadbare USC Trojans T-shirt — the one Kristi loved to sleep in when she spent the night — and nearly lost it.

"Stop it," Shayla ordered herself.

It wasn't as if she would never see them again. Seattle was only a plane ride away. She could make it back here twice a month if necessary.

But she knew that wouldn't happen.

How many times had Braylon asked her — begged her — to come home? She could never find the time. There was always another project on the horizon, another assignment that could possibly move her closer to the top. Shayla knew if she went back to Seattle, she'd fall right back into her old way of life in no time at all.

She pictured Kristi, with her precious smile that was now missing a tooth. And Cassidy, who was just learning to find her smile again. Those girls had come to mean the world to her. How much would it hurt them if she left? How much would it hurt *her*?

Shayla plopped down on the bed next to

the suitcase. She set her elbows on her knees and covered her face in her hands.

"You don't want to do this," she said.

Xavier was right. She belonged in Gauthier. She'd carved out a life for herself here. She had a thriving business to run, two nieces she adored and a man who loved her.

Nothing in Seattle could compete with what Gauthier offered. Here, she had the life she never knew she'd always wanted.

Shayla's head popped up at the sound of knocking at the back door. She pushed up from the bed and trudged toward the kitchen. She opened the back door, expecting to find Xavier. Instead, she found Leslie.

"Can I come in?"

Shayla just stared for a moment. After what had happened yesterday, she was certain Leslie would never want to speak to her again.

"Shayla?"

"Yes. Yes, of course." Shayla shook her head. "Come in." She opened the door wider to let Leslie inside. "Do you . . . uh . . . want some coffee?"

"Please." Leslie nodded. "I can use it. I've been up all night."

Anxiety flooded Shayla's bloodstream.

"Why? It is the girls? Is one of them sick?"

"No, no." Leslie looked up, her eyes brimmed with tears. "I've been up all night trying to figure out how to apologize to you." A stream of tears started flowing down her cheeks. "Shayla, I'm so sorry. I never should have said the things I said to you."

Shayla wrapped her arms around her. "It's okay."

"No." Leslie shook her head. "No, it's not. It was wrong and hateful and you didn't deserve it." She swiped at her eyes with the back of her hand. "You didn't deserve it, Shayla."

As hurtful as Leslie's words had been yesterday, her apology this morning was just as assuaging. The ache that had taken up residence in Shayla's chest started to lessen.

She tore a paper towel from the roll that hung underneath the kitchen cabinet and handed it to her sister-in-law.

"Thank you," Leslie said, dabbing at her eyes and nose. "I . . ." She hiccupped. "I was looking for someone to blame for Braylon's death . . . because I . . . I didn't want to blame the only person who was responsible for it."

"Him," Shayla said.

Leslie nodded. "I'm so angry with him. I'm so angry that he didn't get the help he needed. That he left me and the girls."

Shayla rubbed her hand up and down Leslie's arm, trying to provide whatever comfort she could. Her own cheeks were soaked with the torrent of tears flooding her face. She couldn't speak for several minutes, her throat locked up with pain so fierce it resonated throughout her body.

"It's okay to be angry," Shayla finally managed to get out. "It's okay."

"I lied yesterday," Leslie said. She looked up at her again, and the raw pain Shayla saw staring back at her tore her heart in two. "I don't want to raise these girls on my own. I know I can if I have to, but I want you here, Shayla. You have a connection to Braylon that I never had. You know a side of him that I never did, and I want Kristi and Cass to know that side of their father. I want you in their lives. They need you."

Shayla couldn't speak. She tried, but the words just would not make it past the lump of emotion lodged in her throat.

Finally, after several attempts, she said, "I need them, too."

She grabbed another paper towel and blotted her cheeks. "I never knew how much I needed them until I came back to Gauthier. When I think of all the time I missed with them. And now . . ." Her voice broke. "Now . . . I can't imagine my life without them."

"I know they feel the same way. Just look at how you were able to get Cassidy to open up."

Shayla grabbed Leslie's arm. "I'm so sorry about what happened at the campout." Her sister-in-law shook her head, but Shayla continued. "I had no right to say anything to Cassidy about having the birthmark removed without talking it over with you first. You're the only one who makes decisions about the girls' health."

"Except you were right," Leslie said.

Shayla's spine went rigid with shock. "Me?"

Leslie nodded. "I wasn't thinking about what was best for Cassidy. When I look at that birthmark, I see Braylon. It's like a piece of him that he left with her and I thought getting rid of it would be like getting rid of him."

"Oh, God, Les." Shayla brought a hand to her mouth to hold back her sob. It wasn't until that very moment that she understood the true agony her sister-in-law had been quietly going through all these months.

"But I can't do that to Cassidy," Leslie continued. A sad, resigned smile crossed her lips. "As much as I want to hold tight to every piece of Braylon that remains on this earth, I can't let Cass suffer if getting the birthmark removed will make life easier for her. It's bad enough she has to go through life without her father. I just want to make things as easy as possible for them." She looked up at her. "And a big part of that is having their aunt Shayla in their lives."

She pulled Leslie close and wrapped her arms around her.

"Their aunt Shayla is here," she said. "And she isn't going anywhere."

Shayla crossed Main Street carrying a thermos of coffee that she'd brewed at home. She'd tried calling Xavier, but either he was too busy at work, or he was ignoring her call. Shayla refused to believe the latter. Xavier didn't play games. That was one of the things she loved best about him.

If she'd listened to him this morning, she wouldn't be on her way to him right now with a giant mea culpa.

The first thing she noticed when she crossed over to Cooper Lane was the crowd of cars parked in front of the health clinic. This couldn't be good.

Shayla quickened her pace. She climbed up the steps and entered the building, find- ing the lobby crowded with kids with thick red patches on their faces.

Malinda came into the lobby looking harried.

"What's going on here?" Shayla asked.

"Fifth-grade science class went exploring for bugs in the woods behind the school. Apparently a swarm of butterflies led them straight to a huge patch of poison sumac. It was too much for the school nurse to handle by herself, so here we are."

Bianca Charles looked up from the child whose face she was rubbing with thick pink lotion. She had a red patch on her face, too. She shrugged. "They were pretty butterflies."

Shayla sent her an understanding smile. She turned to Malinda. "I assume Xavier is pretty busy with all of this, huh?"

"I've got this covered. He's in the break room chatting with Matt. Go on back there."

Shayla headed for the employee break room. When she came upon the door, she saw Matt and Xavier shaking hands.

"You don't know how much this means to Gauthier," Matt said.

"Actually, I do," Xavier said. "The people here show me every day."

Both men turned to her.

Shayla waved. "Hi."

A brilliant smile lit up Xavier's face. "Hi."

"Am I interrupting something?" she asked.

"Not at all," Matt said. "You're just in time to say hello to the new director and head physician at the Gauthier Health Clinic. We got the funding, and Xavier just agreed to run it."

Shayla clamped her hands together and ran over to Xavier. She wrapped her arms around his neck. "Congratulations!"

"Thank you." He reached behind her and shook Matt's hand. "And thanks again, Matt. I'm looking forward to it."

"Why don't we meet for dinner once you're done here? We have a lot to discuss."

Xavier nodded. "I'll come over to the law firm."

"So, you've officially accepted the job?" Shayla asked once Matt was gone. "You're really staying?"

"I'm staying," he said. "Are you?"

"Yes." She nodded. "I called the company and declined their invitation to interview."

Xavier blew out a rush of air as he snatched her and crushed her to his chest. He closed his mouth over hers in a bruising, almost desperate kiss.

"Thank God," he said. "I thought I would have to take drastic action, like locking you up in your house or something. I didn't want it to come to that."

Shayla choked on her laugh. "No, having you commit a felony would not be a good thing. You're the official town doctor now. You have a reputation to uphold."

He peered down at her. "What made you change your mind?"

"Leslie came to see me this morning. We had the heart-to-heart talk about Braylon that we probably should have had the first day I moved back to Gauthier." She sucked in a deep breath and let it out slowly. "You were right, Xavier. I've put too much into building my relationship with my family. I'm not giving up on it, no matter how difficult things become."

"You don't have to worry about things being difficult. You have someone here to help you through the rough times now."

"Do you know how amazing it makes me feel, knowing you'll be here forever?"

He dipped his head and spoke softly against her lips. "It can't be as amazing as it makes me feel knowing the same thing about you."

EPILOGUE

Shayla put two fingers between her lips and attempted to whistle. "Way to go, Cass!"

Cassidy sent her the thumbs-up sign from where she stood guarding second base. Now that she'd started treatments to remove her birthmark, she exhibited a confidence Shayla had never seen in her before. She could not be any prouder of her niece.

Shayla sat back down on the bleacher, and Xavier wrapped one arm around her, pulling her up against him.

"That was a good play, right?" she asked him.

"Yeah, but that was the most pathetic whistle I've ever heard in my life."

Shayla poked him in the side with her elbow. "I never learned to whistle," she said. "Maybe I'll get one of those knocker thingies like Kristi has. Hey, Kristi —"

"You can't have my knocker," her niece said, stretching the toy out of Shayla's reach.

Xavier chuckled. "I guess you'd better practice your whistling."

"Kristi, didn't we talk about sharing?" Leslie asked.

"It's okay." Shayla affected a pout. "I guess I won't be able to cheer for Cassidy. Then she'll be sad, and I'll be sad. Everyone will just be so sad."

Kristi's gaze narrowed with suspicion. "Okay," she said, handing Shayla the plastic clapping hands. "But you can't keep 'em."

Shayla's head flew back with a laugh.

"Come here." She picked Kristi up and set her in her lap. "We can cheer Cass on together."

All four of them started chanting Cassidy's name. She looked over from second base and waved, a gorgeous smile lighting up her face. Never in her wildest dreams had Shayla imagined she could derive such joy from a simple smile. But that smile had been a long time coming. For all of them.

The new understanding she now had with Leslie had made all the difference over the past couple of months since the Bayou Campers campout. These days they talked about Braylon often. Shayla shared stories of him as a child, and pointed out the myriad ways the girls — especially Kristi — reminded her of him. It felt good to talk about him and remember all the good times they'd shared. In her heart, she knew Braylon would approve.

"Mommy, I need to pee!" Kristi said in a voice loud enough for their entire bleacher section to hear. She seemed oblivious to the laughs from the crowd as she wiggled off Shayla's lap and took Leslie's hand.

"Can you bring me back a Coke from the concession stand?" Shayla called.

Leslie acknowledged her with a wave as she and Kristi marched down the bleachers.

"Uh-oh," Xavier said. "The one who got the base hit in the second inning is up to bat again. I think she's gunning for our girl." He stood and cupped his hands around his mouth. "Watch out for the grounder, Cass!"

Shayla looked up at him and grinned. "You're really into this, aren't you?"

"Hey, that's my protégé out there." He sat back down and rested his elbows on his thighs, his face the picture of concentration. But then he glanced over at her and grinned. "Besides, you promised us all two scoops of ice cream at Hannah's if the Lions win. I want my two scoops."

The crack of the bat rented the air as the batter sent the ball arcing across the field. Shayla's breath suspended as she watched it head straight for Cassidy.

"Come on, Cass. Come on, Cass," she murmured in fervent prayer.

Cassidy set her glove up and the softball fell directly into it.

"Yes!" Shayla shot out of her seat and pumped her fists in the air. "All right, Cass!"

"Good job, Cassidy!" Xavier yelled.

The Lions softball team jogged toward the dugout as Cassidy's catch brought the fourth inning to a close.

"Oh, yeah, baby," Xavier said as Shayla resumed her seat. "We're definitely getting two scoops today!"

She laughed. "No matter the outcome, I promise you'll get however many scoops you want." She took his hand and pressed a kiss to the back of his fingers. "It's the least I can do to pay you back for how happy you've made me."

Never one to shy away from public displays of affection, Xavier leaned over and connected his mouth to hers.

"How should I pay you back for how happy you've made me?" he asked.

Shayla smiled against his lips. "Oh, I'm sure if we put our heads together we can think of something."

ABOUT THE AUTHOR

Farrah Rochon had dreams of becoming a fashion designer as a teenager, until she discovered she would be expected to wear something other than jeans to work every day. Thankfully, the coffee shop where she writes does not have a dress code.

When Farrah is not penning stories, the avid sports fan feeds her addiction to football by attending New Orleans Saints games.

The employees of Thorndike Press hope you have enjoyed this Large Print book. All our Thorndike, Wheeler, and Kennebec Large Print titles are designed for easy reading, and all our books are made to last. Other Thorndike Press Large Print books are available at your library, through selected bookstores, or directly from us.

For information about titles, please call:
  (800) 223-1244

or visit our Web site at:
  http://gale.cengage.com/thorndike

To share your comments, please write:
  Publisher
  Thorndike Press
  10 Water St., Suite 310
  Waterville, ME 04901